DESPERATE MAN

DESPERATE MAN

Wayne D. Overholser

Chivers Press ● G.K. Hall & Co.
Bath, England ● Thorndike, Maine USA

This Large Print edition is published by Chivers Press, England, and by G.K. Hall & Co., USA.

Published in 1998 in the U.K. by arrangement with Golden West Literary Agency.

Published in 1998 in the U.S. by arrangement with Golden West Literary Agency.

U.K. Hardcover ISBN 0–7540–3138–1 (Chivers Large Print)
U.S. Softcover   ISBN 0–7838–8294–7 (Nightingale Collection Edition)

The text of this Large Print edition is unabridged.
Other aspects of the book may vary from the original edition.

Set in 16 pt. New Times Roman.

Printed in Great Britain on acid-free paper.

British Library Cataloguing in Publication Data available

Library of Congress Cataloging-in-Publication Data

Overholser, Wayne D., 1906–
    Desperate man / Wayne D. Overholser.
        p.   cm.
    ISBN 0–7838–8294–7 (large print : sc : alk. paper)
    1. Large type books.   I. Title.
[PS3529.V33D47   1998]
813'.54—dc21   97–35648

For Claire and Robert Athearn

CHAPTER ONE

My father and I were working on the corral gate when I saw my brother Gil riding across the pasture from Bess Nordine's ranch. I said, 'Gil's coming, Pa.' My father tossed his saw on the ground and straightened up. One thing about Gil: when he was on a horse, he was worth watching.

Gil was riding Tuck, his big sorrel gelding. Tuck was the fastest horse in Dillon's Park, and Gil loved him, but loving him wasn't enough to keep Gil from riding hell out of him. Now Tuck was coming in a dead run, Gil sitting nice and easy in the saddle. He put the sorrel over the barbed wire fence between Nordine's Anchor and our Big Ten in a long, graceful jump, and came right on, never missing a lick. A minute later he rode around our barn and reined up in front of us.

My father said, in his mild way, 'In a hurry, Gil?'

'Sure am,' Gil said. 'Saddle up. A bunch of Rafter 3 cows are coming into the park, and we're gonna run 'em back over the hill.'

'Who is?'

'Me 'n' you and Bess and her crew.'

Bess Nordine's crew consisted of two men, Barney Lux and Shorty Quinn. Any way you counted it, that added up to five, including Bess, who was, as Pa often said, the best man in the park. My father was a good hand with a gun and everybody knew it, but even quality wasn't enough against numbers, and Rafter 3 had numbers besides being a plenty salty outfit.

'What happens if we run into some Rafter 3 riders?' my father asked.

'We'll blow their heads off,' Gil said.

He sat looking at Pa, his black Stetson cocked at a rakish angle. Flashy! That was the word for Gil. He could do a lot of things well— almost everything except work. He had a talent for wearing fancy clothes and he owned the most expensive pair of Justins in the park. He always carried a pearl-handled .44 and he was fast and accurate with it; but whether he could kill a man was something else.

Gil had fallen in love with Bess when we first moved to the park three years ago, and he said he was going to marry her. If he did it would be quite a trick, because she was a strong-minded woman from away back. I hoped he got her. It would serve him right.

My father didn't say anything. Impatiently, Gil said, 'Bess told me she'd wait for you.' He motioned toward me. 'The kid can finish the gate.' Then he whirled his sorrel and took off for Anchor.

The kid can finish the gate. That was like him. I stood watching him until he disappeared, blood pounding in my temples. Sure, I could

2

stay here and finish the gate, working my tail off while he sashayed around over the country trying to look good in front of Bess.

Gil was twenty-two. I was nineteen. He used to whip me regularly until I was sixteen. It hadn't been too tough a job, with him three years older than I was. Then there'd been the time in Buhl, the county seat, when he jumped me. I'd have whipped him if Ma hadn't knocked me groggy by hitting me on the head with a frying pan. He hadn't tackled me since.

When Gil was home he never turned a hand. He was sickly, Ma said, and him as big as a young Shorthorn bull, and filled with the same notions every time he looked at Bess. Funny thing: he couldn't work at home, but he'd go over to Bess's ranch and shine up to her.

It was Gil's fault we had to fix the gate. Yesterday he'd been breaking horses for Bess and he'd brought her big black gelding to our place. I think he was scared and didn't want Bess to see him ride the black. He had cause to be scared. The horse took off like a locomotive. He swapped ends; he pawed at the sky; he bucked in short, jolting pitches that snapped Gil's head back and forth until it looked as if it were going to come off; then the black went up in the air and fell over backward.

Gil jumped clear and climbed the corral like a squirrel. I think the horse would have killed him if he'd stayed inside. The black slammed into the gate, busted it all to hell, and took off

3

across the pasture. Good thing Gil hadn't been over at Anchor. He looked bad, with dust all over him and blood running down his mouth and chin from his nose; and looking bad in front of Bess was one thing he couldn't stand.

I hadn't realized my father had saddled up until he said, 'Dave.' He stood a few feet from me, holding the reins of his brown horse. When I looked at him, he said, 'I've felt the same way more'n once, Dave.' He stepped into the saddle. Then he said, 'Never mind the gate.'

He rode off, not across the pasture the way Gil had, but down the lane to the road. Quite a man, my father. Big, hard-working, patient, Joe Munro deserved more than he'd ever received from life—the way I saw it, anyhow. He was one of the reasons I'd stayed home. He needed me and he loved me, and I loved him.

I hated Gil. I'd hated him as long as I could remember, and someday I'd break his neck. There were times, too, when I hated my mother. I knew it was wrong, but I couldn't help it. I'd felt that way long before she'd hit me on the head with a frying pan.

Ma hadn't wanted me in the first place. She had a hard time when Gil was born. She almost died, and she told my father she wouldn't have any more children. I was an accident. She didn't make any bones about saying it right out.

I don't believe she ever neglected me—physically, I mean. But I was her duty child and

4

Gil her love child. If she ever gave me a caress or a word of endearment, I couldn't remember it.

'Where did they go, Dave?' Ma called from the back porch.

I stood looking at her for a moment. She was a small woman, under five feet, and I never knew her to weigh more than one hundred pounds. Now, at forty, she was showing her age. Her hair was gray; she had wrinkles in her cheeks and around her eyes; and the backs of her hands were brown with liver spots.

Right then I wasn't in any mood to listen to her fret about Gil. I said, 'A bunch of Rafter 3 cows are headed into the park, and they're going to run 'em back over the hill.'

Now she really had something to fret about. All of us who lived in the park were under the shadow of Rafter 3 guns. The trouble had never come to a head, but it was only a question of time until it would, unless Vic Toll, the Rafter 3 foreman, got a dose of lead poisoning.

I went into the barn, climbed to the mow, and lay down on the hay. I had a hunch Kitsy would be over. She was Bess's younger sister, seventeen and pretty, and the one person in the world who meant more to me than my father. We were in love and wanted to get married, but Bess threw the monkey wrench at us.

Bess was twenty-five, and she and Kitsy had no one but each other. Their folks died when

Kitsy was small and Bess had practically raised her. 'Kitsy isn't going to work like I have,' Bess said flatly. 'When she's eighteen, she's going away to school. She'll marry somebody with money, not a kid like you, Dave, who doesn't have ten cents to his name.'

Bess wasn't a woman to change her mind. She didn't have anything against me, but she'd decided Kitsy's future, and that ended the whole business.

The only time Kitsy and I were alone was when Bess and the crew were gone, and Gil wasn't at either place. Oh, we could see each other, at parties or in church on Sunday morning or maybe at a school shindig, but always when Bess was around, so we sneaked off to be together when we got a chance, and this was too good to miss.

I didn't wait long. I heard the barn door open and close, the one on the north side that Ma couldn't see from the house. A moment later Kitsy climbed the ladder to the mow and stood there, smiling provocatively at me.

I said, 'Hello, Kitsy.'

She put her hands on her hips. 'Were you expecting me?'

I said, 'Counting on it.'

I couldn't even look at her without getting tied up inside. Blue eyes, chestnut hair that held just a little curl, a slim figure more girl than woman, Kitsy Nordine was everything in the world I wanted. Maybe I didn't have ten cents

6

to my name, but it didn't matter: being in love was enough.

Without any warning Kitsy dived at me. She fell on top of me, knocking the breath out of my lungs. She tickled me under my arms until I shoved her off, then she clenched her fists and twisted them back and forth against the sides of my head.

'Quit it,' I said, 'or I'll bust you one.'

'Go on,' she challenged. 'Bust me.'

I got on top of her and pinned her arms down on both sides of her. 'All right,' I said. 'I don't know why I always have to prove I'm bigger than you are.'

'Bigger,' she jeered. 'What does that prove? All muscles and no brain.'

There was only one way to win an argument with Kitsy. I kissed her, and her arms came around me. Her hands weren't clenched now, but open and soft, gently caressing me. I rolled off her and we lay beside each other, breathing hard. We were silent a long time. Just being together was enough. We gave each other the love that neither of us had ever had before, and it was sweet and beautiful and utterly wonderful.

CHAPTER TWO

Kitsy went to sleep on my arm, as she often did when we were alone this way. Then, for some reason, old memories came alive in my mind, and I thought how it had been, back over the years that made us Munros what we were, that made me feel about Gil the way I did.

We had been drifters until we came to the park, moving any place where my father could find work. Sometimes his gun was the tool he used to make a living. He had been a lawman of different kinds, shotgun guard on a stage, and night watchman at mines in the high country; but they were always temporary jobs. Usually he took anything he could get.

My mother worked as hard as my father. Like Pa, she was capable of doing almost anything from keeping house to teaching school. I worked, too, as far back as I could remember: running errands, selling papers, and even cleaning out a livery stable when I was so small I couldn't handle a loaded wheelbarrow.

Gil was the only one who hadn't worked.

*   *   *

My parents never talked about their background, but I knew they'd come from

8

Ohio and were married when they were young. They left home because my father's folks had forbidden the marriage. When they moved to Colorado hard times gripped the country, and I guess they almost starved to death for a few years.

Both of my parents had their dreams, stemming out of those terrible years of privation. My mother, always a worrier, wanted money. We saved every dollar we could, often going without things we needed so that another five-dollar gold piece could go into the little box my father had ingeniously hidden in the covered wagon.

My mother was always vague about why she wanted the money. When my father pinned her down, she'd say: 'Someday we're going to be too old to work for other people. Then we'll buy a store.' But I thought she wanted to give it to Gil, when he was twenty-one, to start him in business. If she had, he'd have blown it in a poker game or on a fine horse and saddle, or anything that happened to strike his fancy.

Money had no value to my father unless it was used to buy something we could use. In his eyes land was the only real security. 'People can steal money,' he'd say to my mother, 'but the Lord made the land. It'll be here long after we're gone.'

My mother would sniff disdainfully. 'If you don't pay your taxes,' she'd say, 'they take your land away from you. Or if you borrow money from the bank, they take your land when you don't pay the interest. The worst robbers in the country are the bankers and tax collectors.'

The argument went on and on, through all those years of drifting. But while the money was piling up slowly, my father never forgot his dream. As we wandered through the San Luis Valley or along the Uncompahgre or up the Grand, he would sometimes pull his brown horse to a stop, his gaze on a ranch house beside the road, the hay meadows along a river, or the long slopes behind the house that reached up to the spruce and aspens.

If my mother and Gil were with us, he'd never say anything. He'd just look, a strange expression in his gray eyes, as if he had forgotten he had a family, and, for the moment, thought he was a free man, living the way he wanted to live, with his roots going down into the good rich soil.

If we were alone, he'd say: 'That's the kind of ranch we're going to own some day, Dave: a tight house and a barn and corrals, with summer range reaching clean back to the sky and haystacks along the river and a thousand head of cattle grazing all summer up there on the mesa, with our brand on them. Our brand.' Then he'd shake his head and look at me, with a funny little grin under his bristly mustache. 'Don't tell Ma we seen this ranch. We'll just remember it.'

The ranches we were supposed to remember were scattered all over the eastern plains and the western slope. But, oddly enough, when my father bought a ranch it wasn't one we were going to remember, but one none of us but Pa had seen.

That was three years ago, the fall I was sixteen and Gil was nineteen. My father and I had worked a good part of the summer on White River putting up hay; my mother cooked for the hay crew, and as usual, Gil found some reason to keep from working, though he was well enough to win the bucking contest in the Fourth of July rodeo.

When we were done haying, my father and mother had a wrangle about where we'd go. Ma wanted to head south where the winter wouldn't be as tough as it would in the northern part of the state, but Pa insisted we'd go north and take a look at the town of Buhl. He won, simply by hitching up and driving north. Ma had the choice of riding north or walking south, so she elected to ride.

When we got to Buhl, we camped along the river under some cottonwoods, and Pa and I walked to town. Gil stayed with Ma at the wagon. She always worried about leaving it, with a little better than two thousand dollars laid away in the box. Besides, Gil had a sore throat, and she was going to fix him some onion juice and swab his throat with coal oil.

I was looking forward to seeing the town

11

with my father, but after I took a look at it I wondered why he'd insisted on driving more than seventy miles out of our way just to see a dusty little cowtown. When I asked him, he gave me that funny grin I'd seen so many times and said, 'I've got my reasons.'

We went into the Belle Union saloon and my father had whiskey and I had sarsaparilla. I figured I was big enough for whiskey, but Pa didn't. He finished his drink. Then he said, 'How far is it to Dillon's Park?'

'Forty-three miles,' the barkeep said. 'Head out through the sagebrush till you get to Buck Creek. Cross it and go on. When you get to the Big Red, you're there.'

My father had another drink. Then he asked, 'Ever hear of the Big Ten?'

The bartender squinted at him. Then he said, 'Yeah. Belongs to a widow named Jason. Her husband got plugged three, four months ago. She'll sell it cheap but I hear there ain't no buyers.'

'Why not?'

The bartender polished a glass with a furious motion, scowling as if he wished my father hadn't asked the question. Finally he said, 'I don't know nothing 'bout how Herb Jason got beefed.'

'I didn't ask about Jason,' my father said mildly.

The bartender tipped his head at a table where half a dozen men were playing poker.

12

'See the big gent with the hooked nose and the overgrown chin?'

We looked. You couldn't mistake the man he meant. He was young, maybe twenty-five. He had a hooked nose and an overgrown chin, all right. Even sitting in a chair, he looked like a giant. His face was so dark I thought he was a breed, but afterward my father said No, he was burned that way by being out in the wind and sun. He had a tall pile of chips in front of him, and as we watched he pulled in the chips that were in the middle of the table, said something to the man beside him, and laughed.

'Yeah, I see him,' my father said.

'He's Vic Toll, foreman of the Rafter 3,' the barman said. 'Most of the country you'll cross getting to Dillon's Park is Rafter 3 range. Belongs to a big cowman named Cameron Runyan, who lives in Wyoming. If you want to know why nobody's bought the Big Ten, ask Vic.'

The bartender walked away. I guess he was afraid my father would ask something else. We left the saloon and returned to the wagon, my father looking thoughtful. After a while, he said, 'Don't tell Ma or Gil about what you heard.'

I nodded, and then he said, 'That Vic Toll is a tough hombre. Ain't hard to figure out why nobody wants the Big Ten, but there's some that's lived in the park for years. Maybe we can, too.'

The sun was almost down, and the air was still and hot. It never occurred to me Pa would really buy the Big Ten because I knew what Ma would say.

My father said, 'If a man gets desperate enough, so damned desperate he ain't real sure what he's doing, he'll gamble his life for a dream. I'm going to take a ride, Dave. I'll be gone in the morning. You tell Ma I'll be back in three or four days.'

Sure enough, in the morning he was gone. I told Ma and she had a fit. She hadn't wanted to come here in the first place and she thought we'd be headed south by sunup. The day was a long one, with nothing to do but sit. Gil said, 'Let's hitch up and start south. He'll catch up with us.'

But Ma wouldn't do it. She loved Pa in her peculiar way, I guess. At least she didn't want to give him up. So we waited. The second day was worse than the first, and the third worst of all, with Gil cranky mean and Ma getting jumpier every hour.

Finally Gil picked a fight. I was almost as big as he was, and I wasn't afraid of him any more. I gave him all he wanted, getting through his guard with a good right that knocked him clean over the bank to the gravel bar along the river. Then I jumped on him, pinning him down with my knees, and I hammered him on the face with one fist and then the other, with Ma screaming at me to quit picking on him.

14

That was when she hit me with the frying pan.

Ma was strong, even if she didn't weigh over ninety-eight pounds. Gil pushed me off, and when I got up, the river was spinning around like a silver wheel. He finished me then. When I came to, Pa was there.

Ma was still so mad she was white in the face. 'Did I raise two boys to fight like a pair of dogs?' she shouted. 'Don't you ever strike Gil again! You hear, Dave?'

I guess Pa had just ridden up. He took Ma by the shoulders and looked down at her. He said, 'I've seen a lot of these rows start, and I never knew Dave to be to blame.'

'You always take Dave's side,' she cried. 'Gil's got a sore throat—'

'Sadie,' my father said in a low voice, 'Gil is a God-damned lazy parasite. From now it'll be different or you can take Gil and start down the road.'

'All right, I'll get the money and—'

'No,' my father said. 'I spent all the money but $12.42 buying a ranch in Dillon's Park. It's a good ranch: two hundred head under the Big Ten iron, a tight little house, with a river just across the road and hay meadows and summer range on Campbell Mountain.'

For a moment she stood there, white-faced, and then she began to curse him. He put a hand over her mouth. He said, 'Shut up or I'll put you across my knee and paddle some sense into your butt. If you want to leave me, go ahead.

15

I'd be better off with a woman who'd be a wife to me.' He shoved her away as if he couldn't stand the sight of her.

She fainted, the only time in my life I ever saw her faint. Ma was much better after that. He should have whittled her down a long time ago, but he was a gentle man by nature and only a crazy fury would have made him talk to her that way.

I'll never forget my first sight of the Big Ten with its white four-room house, barn, and corrals, and Campbell Mountain heaving up against the sky on the east. The Big Red curled down from the north and the great sandstone cliff rose a sheer five hundred feet above the river. There were cottonwoods between the house and the road. None of the big ranches my father had said to remember compared to the Big Ten.

I remembered Pa saying that when a man got desperate enough, he'd gamble his life for his dream. He had, right here on the Big Ten for three years, and nothing had happened. We were the closest ranch in the park to the Rafter 3. If the trouble ever came to a head, we'd get hit first.

The old-timers, like Elder Smith, who was teacher, preacher, storekeeper, and postmaster at the settlement up the river which really wasn't a settlement at all, told us that the smell of trouble had been in the air for years. Rafter 3 cattle had always wintered in the park, but now that park ranchers had made clear their intention to keep them out, anything could happen.

*　　　*　　　*

Kitsy woke up and yawned. 'Was I asleep?'

'Sure. Snored your head off.'

She laughed. 'You fool, I don't snore, but you do. I don't know if I ever want to sleep with you all night or not.'

'Sure you do. You've wanted to sleep all night with me ever since I came here.'

She made a face at me and sat up. She began picking hay off her dress as she said: 'I was only fourteen and you were sixteen—just kids, but we knew right from the start. Now we're old. Seventeen and nineteen. Let's not waste our lives. Marry me, Dave.'

'I'm going to.'

'Tomorrow?'

'No.'

'When, Dave?'

'I don't know,' I said miserably.

I heard my mother's fretful voice, 'Dave? Dave, where are you?'

'I've got to go see what she wants,' I said.

We went down the ladder and walked in front of the mangers to the other side of the barn. I helped her down into a stall. I looked at her, my hands gripping her arms, and I saw how much she wanted me; it was in her eyes, in

17

the tremulous smile on her lips.

'I love you, Kitsy,' I said. 'It's like—It's like being out in the cold, dark night, with just one big star in the sky. You're that star, and you always will be.'

'Dave,' she whispered. 'Dave.'

I kissed her, and then she whirled from me and ran out of the barn. I closed the door and walked along the runway, feeling the blood pounding in my head. How desperate had my father been, that time three years ago when he'd gone against my mother and bought the Big Ten?

CHAPTER THREE

By the time I finished the chores, it was completely dark. I stood on the back porch and smoked a cigarette. My mother was in the pantry straining the milk and pouring it into pans so she could skim it in the morning. When she was done, she came out of the kitchen and sat down on the porch.

Ma was hoping to catch the sound of incoming horses, I thought, but there was only the silence of a vast and nearly empty country. She was worried about Gil. I pondered that for a time, thinking how she wanted him to have anything he wanted, even to marrying Bess.

Gil proposed to Bess whenever he had a

chance, but she kept putting him off, so Ma went over to see her. Kitsy was in the kitchen and heard the conversation. She said Ma had told Bess that Gil was eating his heart out and what kind of a woman was she, turning down a good boy like that?

Bess didn't pussyfoot around any. She said her husband would have to be a better man than she was and Gil hadn't proved he was. Then she came right out and said she wouldn't have her mother-in-law telling her how to treat her husband. Ma got up and walked out. She hadn't liked Bess since then.

When I finished my cigarette, I said, 'I'm hungry.'

'I'll cook a hot supper soon as they get here,' Ma said.

I walked across the yard to the barn, thinking how Gil had ridden up to the corral and called me 'kid' and said I could finish the gate. All of a sudden I decided I'd had enough. I was going to pull out.

A few minutes later I heard them coming. I stayed in the shadows until they took care of their horses. When they started toward the house, I called, 'Pa.'

They wheeled, and Gil said in that contemptuous way he had, 'Oh, it's the kid.'

I started toward him, but my father stepped in front of me, saying, 'Gil, go tell your mother we're here.'

My brother grunted something and walked

19

away. I said, 'Someday I'm going to break his God-damned neck.'

'Not tonight,' my father said. 'What's on your mind, Dave?'

'I'm leaving,' I said. 'I wanted to tell you good-bye.'

'Tell me about it,' he said quietly.

There wasn't much to tell, less than I thought when I tried to put it into words. I was just sick of getting the skim milk and Gil taking the cream.

'Is this on account of a busted-up corral gate?' my father asked.

'It's more than that,' I said.

'I won't beg you to stay, if this is what you've got to do, but I think I've got a right to ask you to put off leaving until tomorrow night. I'm going to Buhl in the morning to talk to Cameron Runyan. I hear he's in town. I'm not sure I can do any good, but there'll be hell to pay in the park this winter if we don't do something.'

'You don't need me to talk to Runyan.'

'Did you ever run away from a fight, Dave?'

'I don't think so.'

'There'll be a fight,' he said. 'Maybe not tomorrow, but sometime. What I've got to find out is whether Runyan backs Toll all the way. We chased the Rafter 3 cows across Buck Creek; then we ran into a couple of Toll's men, and Bess shot one of 'em. That means we'll be seeing Vic Toll. Runyan's the only man who

20

can head off the trouble.'

'All right, I'll go with you,' I said.

'That's better. Now let's go get our supper.'

After we finished eating, Pa said, 'Dave's going to town with me in the morning. Gil, you fix the corral gate while we're gone.' He nodded at me. 'Better roll in, Dave.'

It was still dark when he called me in the morning. We wolfed our breakfast and went out into the cold, still air. There was no sign of the sun, but the sky was clear, and the moon, well over to the west now, washed the earth with its pale light. We went down the lane to the county road, then swung east. We crossed Buck Creek, made the long climb to the plateau above the park, and struck off across it toward Buhl. The sun was up then, and we rode directly into the sharp, slanting rays.

This was Rafter 3 range, a rolling sagebrush plain with patches of greasewood here and there, and an occasional cedar. The air was cold with a biting wind that drove through my sheepskin and chilled me to the bone.

Vic Toll and his boss, Cameron Runyan, had reason enough to want Dillon's Park for winter range. The grass was better in the park than here on the plateau, but the main difference was a matter of weather. Spring came a month earlier along the river than up here where the wind was either Arctic cold or oven hot. Rafter 3 had heavy winter loss; we had very little.

I asked myself what chance we had against the power of a man like Cameron Runyan, especially when Vic Toll was doing Runyan's fighting for him. If we ran into Vic Toll today, we'd be dead men.

Part of the trouble was that the sheriff, fat Ed Veach, walked a tightrope trying to satisfy the townsmen in Buhl, the small ranchers scattered all over the country, and Cameron Runyan. Actually, he satisfied no one, unless it was Runyan, and I wasn't even sure about that.

I felt the heavy weight of the gun against my side. My father had told me to wear it. I wasn't as fast with it as Gil, but I was reasonably accurate at close range. Pa had bought it for me the summer we were haying on White River because he got it cheap. It was a Peacemaker, a .45 with a three-inch barrel. It had the old style one-piece wood grips, and no ejector, a gun nobody else wanted, I guess, but I was used to it.

Pa had made Gil and me put in hours of practice, particularly after we came to the park. 'You never know what you're going to do until you're up against it,' he'd said several times. 'Facing a man with a gun in his hand ain't like shooting at a tin can. Some men have a quality that makes 'em stand and fight; others cave.'

I tried to pin him down as to what that quality was, but he couldn't put it into words. 'Call it x,' he said. 'It's not just the sand in a man's craw. I've seen good fist fighters who couldn't stand up against a gun.'

I'd often wondered if I had the quality he called *x*. 'It's the first time that counts,' Pa often said. 'If you run then, chances are you'll always run.' This was my first time, and I had a hunch he'd thought of that when he'd asked me to come with him.

I glanced at him. He had a strong, high-boned face, with a sharp nose and wide chin and heavy lips. I wondered why he had been a drifter instead of making a career out of being a law man. I asked, 'Why didn't you become a U.S. Marshal or something like that?'

He gave me a sharp glance and then stared straight ahead. 'Your mother always nagged me when I took a job of that kind so I quit.' He chewed on his lower lip a moment, and then added: 'I guess I didn't want that kind of life enough to fight her. I wasn't desperate enough.'

That was his favorite word. If you were *desperate* enough, he'd say, you can always do the job that needs to be done. Then I had the answer to the question I'd asked myself awhile ago. If we were desperate enough; we could hold the park against Rafter 3.

'There's one thing I didn't mention last night,' my father went on. 'The Big Ten will make a living for you and Kitsy. I mean, I hope it'll work that way. Gil's not the kind who would appreciate it.'

Hope flared up in me. If I told Bess I could take Kitsy to the Big Ten and make a living for her there, she might change her mind. The next thought killed that hope as quickly as it had come to me. No woman, not even Kitsy, could live on the Big Ten with my mother.

We rode in silence again until, in early afternoon, we saw the buildings of Buhl ahead of us. I finally asked the question that had been bothering me from the time we'd left home. 'Why do you figure we'll have trouble this winter with Rafter 3?'

'Several reasons.' He threw out a hand in a wide gesture. 'We had a dry year last summer. This is the poorest graze I ever saw for a big outfit, so they need the park worse than they ever have before. Another thing is what we done yesterday. Bess says from now on there'll never be another Rafter 3 critter on our graze, so to make it look tough, she threw a little lead. Toll won't overlook it.'

On Saturdays Buhl was a buzzing town unless the weather was bad, but this was the middle of the week. No one was in sight. Except for a dog dozing in the sun and a scraggly rooster that was scratching up a dust cloud at the other end of Main Street, the town appeared deserted.

We turned into a livery stable, my father asking as we swung down, 'Cameron Runyan in town?'

'Still here.' The hostler nodded at a pair of

matched bays in neighboring stalls. 'That's his team. Never knew him to ride a saddle horse. Always riding behind that team when he comes to Buhl. He don't go no place where they can't take him.'

I followed my father down the runway to a horse trough in the back. We washed up, then my father glanced at the sun. 'After noon,' he said, 'but he still might be having dinner.'

We went back through the runway. Just before we reached the street, the hostler called, 'Joe.' My father turned. 'You're packing a gun. Never saw you wear one before.' He motioned toward me. 'So's Dave. What's up?'

'Nothing—I hope.'

My father started toward the street, but stopped again when the hostler said, 'Something you ought to know, Joe.'

'Toll in town?' my father asked.

'No, but Runyan's got a couple of gun hands with him.'

'Who are they?'

'A little gent named Sammy Blue. Didn't catch the other one's name.'

'Thanks, Mike,' my father said, and this time the hostler let him go.

I'd never heard of Sammy Blue and I asked my father about him. He shrugged. 'He's a gunslinger. I met up with him in Durango nine, ten years ago.'

Before we went into the hotel, my father said in a low voice: 'Watch it, Dave. This may be

25

tight.'

We crossed the lobby to the desk. My father asked, 'Cameron Runyan staying here?'

'He's registered here,' the clerk answered.

'What's his room number?'

'He's not in his room. I believe he's in the dining room.'

'Thanks,' my father said.

A man who had been sitting in a rawhide-bottom chair in the far corner of the lobby got up and started toward us. As my father turned toward the dining-room door, the man said, 'Who wants to see Mr. Runyan?'

'I do,' my father said.

The stranger came on across the lobby. He was a little man, not more than five feet three, maybe four, inches, and slender. The gun on his right hip looked too big for him to handle, but I had a hunch he could handle it fast and well. He had a short, wide face with a high forehead so that his features in the bottom half of his face had the appearance of being squished together.

This, I thought, must be Sammy Blue.

CHAPTER FOUR

My Father and Sammy Blue faced each other for what was probably not more than a few seconds, certainly less than a minute, but to me it was much longer. My hand was on my gun butt. I don't know why, because I knew I couldn't interfere as long as this was strictly between my father and Blue. My gaze moved from my father's pale face to the gunman's, and I saw that Sammy was puzzled.

'I'll be damned.' Blue laughed and held out his hand. 'I thought I ought to know you. You're Joe Munro, ain't you?'

'That's right, Sammy,' my father said, and shook his hand.

Blue stepped back, the laughter leaving his face. 'Been a long time.'

'A long time,' my father agreed.

'Didn't know you lived hereabouts,' Blue said. 'Where you holed up?'

I suspected that Blue knew before he asked. He spoke guardedly, as if he had to be sure, and when my father said, 'Dillon's Park,' Sammy Blue's face lost its trace of friendliness.

'I'm sorry to hear that,' Blue said. 'My job is to look out for Mr. Runyan's comfort, and it don't take no smart man to see that you aim to make him uncomfortable.'

'I aim to see him,' my father said. 'We got up uncommonly early and made a hell of a long ride to see him.'

'This your kid?' Blue asked, motioning to me without taking his eyes off my father.

He could see to either side as well as in front, I thought, and I had a hunch that any fast action on my part, even standing at an angle from him as I was, would bring a blazing gun out of his holster. He reminded me of a pugnacious cat, taut-muscled and graceful, waiting for a mouse to make his move.

'He's the young one,' my father said. 'I've got another boy at home.'

'I'm sorry about your long ride,' Blue said, 'but you might as well head back. Mr. Runyan's eating dinner, and he don't want to be bothered. Besides, it wouldn't do you no good. Vic Toll's your man.'

My father didn't budge. He stood there like a rock, and I had never admired him more than I did at that moment. He was desperate, I thought, so desperate that he would see Cameron Runyan or die trying. After all these years, he had what he wanted and he would not give it up.

'Get out of my way, Sammy,' my father said. 'I'm going to see Runyan.'

'I'm telling you otherwise,' Blue said. 'Don't push me, Joe. You ain't the man who can do it and you know it.'

Without taking his eyes off Blue, my father said, 'Dave, go take a look in the dining room. If Runyan's there, tell him I want to see him and ask him when would be a good time.'

'Don't do it, kid,' Blue said. 'I'll drop your dad before you make two steps and then I'll drop you.'

'No, you won't,' the hotel clerk said. 'I've got a double-barreled scatter-gun that's loaded with buckshot. If you two roosters want to kill each other, go out into the street to do it.'

I turned my head enough to see the clerk. He wasn't fooling. He had a shotgun in his hands, all right, and at this distance he'd blow both men apart. Blue said, 'All right, Brown. We'll go outside.'

'No,' my father said. 'I didn't make this ride just for a gun fight. I'm here to see Cameron Runyan and that's what I'm going to do.'

They stood that way for what must have been thirty seconds. I watched them, sweating and trembling and more scared than I had ever been in my life. I don't know what would have happened if Runyan hadn't walked out of the dining room. He asked, 'What's going on here, Sammy?'

I'd never seen Cameron Runyan before, but I'd heard about him and I knew this was Runyan. He was in his middle sixties, an average-looking man in a broadcloth suit with a spade beard and mustache. He didn't look like a cowman. He wasn't even wearing boots. His patent leather shoes were low heeled. To all appearances he might have been a successful storekeeper who liked to eat so well he had gone a little paunchy.

'This fellow rode in from Dillon's Park to see you,' Blue said. 'I told him you didn't want to be bothered.'

'Sometimes you take on too much territory, Sammy,' Runyan said. 'Ever think about asking me if I wanted to be bothered?'

'Didn't figure it was necessary,' Blue said. 'I told Munro that Vic Toll was the man to see.'

'Munro, eh?' Runyan said. 'I've heard of you. Bought Herb Jason's place three years ago, didn't you?' He shook hands with my father, and then with me when my father introduced us. 'Come upstairs to my room.' He motioned toward a big man who had followed him out of the dining room. 'Come along, Mort. Stay here, Sammy.'

He climbed the stairs slowly, holding to the railing with one hand. The man he had called Mort followed close behind. Another bodyguard, I thought. The faithful dog type. He didn't look very bright, but he carried a gun and he was big, and he'd follow orders without asking questions. He was the opposite of Sammy Blue, but, in his own way, just as dangerous.

My father followed Mort, and I brought up the rear. Halfway to the top, I looked down. Blue was standing at the desk, his hands palm down on top of the register. He said, 'You butted in, Brown. I don't like that.' The clerk replied levelly, 'I'm sorry, but I refuse to let you turn my lobby into a shooting gallery.'

I didn't hear any more, but it was enough to prove that all the brave men in the world weren't the ones who packed guns. There weren't many men in Buhl, I thought, who would make a stand against the Rafter 3.

Runyan led the way to his room, opened the door and went in. He took a cigar out of a box on the bureau and sat down in a rocking chair next to a window. Mort stood by the door until my father and I were inside, then he shut the door and stood against it, looking bored with the whole business.

Runyan bit off the end of his cigar and lighted it. He said, 'What's on your mind, Munro?'

He didn't ask us to sit down, so it would be a brief interview. He leaned back in his rocking chair, his cigar held between his teeth, his fat hands folded over his stomach. I was convinced we had made our ride for nothing.

'I think you know,' my father said. 'I came here to ask you to let us alone.'

Runyan seemed amused. 'Friend, I am letting you alone. I'd like to own the park, mind you, and I would own it if it hadn't been settled by some mule-headed men.'

'Like Herb Jason?' my father asked.

'Like Herb Jason,' Runyan agreed. 'His wife, too. She knew I'd pay her any reasonable price for the Big Ten, but she took less money to sell to you. Now if you're worried about the future, Munro, I'll write you out a check today for six thousand dollars. You got it for a third of that. Can a man expect a bigger profit than that?'

'The Big Ten ain't for sale,' my father said.

'Didn't figure it was.' Runyan took the cigar

out of his mouth and inspected the ash.

'I didn't come here to talk about Herb Jason,' my father said. 'I'm the only newcomer in the park, but I'm as mule-headed as the next man. We're small fry, all of us. In the summer we run our stock on Campbell Mountain, and in the park during the winter. Just ten of us. If you add up our herds, we'd make about a quarter of what you've got under the Rafter 3 iron. They tell me that's only one of six outfits you own.'

'That's right,' Runyan agreed. 'Are you saying it's a crime for me to be big while you're little?' He shook his head. 'Poor reasoning, Munro. When I was the age of your boy, I owned my horse and saddle. That was all. I've come a long ways since then, and under my own steam. You can do the same if you have the ability and want to work like I did.'

My father moved toward Runyan until he stood within ten feet of the man. Looking down, he said, 'I know there's no use in talking to Vic Toll. I figured you'd be smarter and you might be a human being. That's why I came to see you. We want to be let alone, Runyan. Is that too much to ask?'

'Have I bothered you?'

'Not yet, but Toll will. We've got wives and children, all of us but Elder Smith and Bess Nordine, and she's got a younger sister who's dependent on her.'

'I know,' Runyan said impatiently. 'Bess

Nordine is the dangerous one, Munro.' He waggled a fat forefinger at my father. 'She'll have you making trouble for us and when she does, you'll get hurt. Sure I'll let you alone, but the question is whether you'll let us alone.' He pulled on his cigar, found that it had gone cold, and took it out of his mouth. 'Strikes me you've done something and you're scared. What is it?'

'We chased some Rafter 3 cows out of the park yesterday, and Bess took a shot at one of your men. We've had a dry year, just like you have, and we're as short of grass as you are. We won't let any of your stock winter in the park.'

'So that's it,' Runyan murmured. 'Now I'll tell you exactly how it is. I've made a success by picking good men to work for me. Vic Toll is one of the best. When he was the age of your boy, he was a top hand. He went to work for me when he was twenty. A year later I made him foreman of the Rafter 3 and I have never regretted it. He's had the job six years, and the Rafter 3 has never failed to show a profit in those six years.'

'You'll back anything he does?'

'I wouldn't put it that way. Let's say that as long as he shows a profit, I won't interfere with the way he runs Rafter 3.'

'You condone murder?'

'Damn it, I didn't say that, either,' Runyan snapped. 'I told you I wouldn't interfere. That's all I've got to say except that I'll buy your ranch and any of the other ranches in the park that are for sale, and I'll pay a good price. Good day, Munro.' He nodded at Mort, who opened the door, then rose and moved to the window, giving us his back as he fumbled in his pocket for a match.

We walked out and the door closed behind us. My father stood staring at the door for a moment, as angry as I had ever seen him. 'The bastard,' he said. 'He pays Vic Toll's wages, but he won't take any responsibility for what he does.'

We went down the stairs and crossed the lobby. We saw Sammy Blue sitting in a chair in the corner, his eyes on us. When we reached the boardwalk, my father paused, glancing back uncertainly. He said, 'Let's go over to the store and buy something to eat. And walk slow.'

We stepped off the boardwalk and started across the street, moving slowly, just as my father had said. Then I heard Sammy Blue call, 'Munro!'

I knew, then, that my father had expected trouble and this was it.

CHAPTER FIVE

If I had been alone I would have turned to look at Blue, and I would probably have died right there in the street if my father hadn't said

34

quickly, 'Keep walking. Take two steps and turn. Pull your gun and shoot the man on your right.'

This was a maneuver my father had made Gil and me practice many times. By turning so that my right side, the side my gun was on, was away from the man behind me, I could make a half turn and face Sammy Blue with my gun in my hand before he knew I had started my draw. At least, that was the way it was supposed to work, if I didn't freeze up.

At the moment I wasn't scared. I suppose I didn't have time. I took the two steps in the same slow pace I had been walking, not sure what had happened, but guessing that Sammy Blue was bent on salving his pride, and that Mort, who had probably followed us down the stairs, had been sucked into the play. Of course, there was a chance that Runyan had ordered us killed, but somehow that didn't seem like him.

Then I was turning, right hand sweeping my gun from holster as I swung around. I was geared to shoot, I couldn't have kept my trigger finger from squeezing off a shot if I had wanted to. Both Blue and Mort were standing in front of the hotel. Blue was on my right, so I took him. My bullet smashed his gun arm and whirled him around, knocking him back against the hotel wall.

Blue had expected us to face him and then be goaded into making a play, so we completely surprised him. He was too slow going for his gun; it wasn't quite level when my bullet knocked it out of his hand. Mort was even slower. His gun wasn't clear of leather when my father's first bullet took him in the stomach, the second in the neck. The slug must have cut his jugular vein. He went down, blood spurting all over the walk. He was dead within a matter of seconds.

'We still may be in trouble,' my father said in a low tone. 'Don't move. We'll have to see how it goes.'

I stood there, my gun dangling at my side, suddenly weak and sweating, my knees threatening to fold under me. Men ran out of the hotel and the store behind us and the Belle Union beside the store. Doc Holt came out of his office, his black bag in his hand, and ran to where Sammy Blue lay on the walk a few feet from Mort.

I had seen gun fights in Durango and Leadville and Trinidad. In my imagination I had seen myself in the street mowing down bank robbers, but it hadn't been like this. Even my wildest dreams had never pitted me against a man like Sammy Blue. Sweat ran down my forehead into my eyes. I wiped my face with the sleeve of my left arm, then I backed up until I could lean against the hitch rail in front of the store.

'Get hold of yourself, Dave,' my father said. 'I don't like the looks of this. Whatever happens, we can't let Veach take us to jail.'

I knew what he meant. Once locked up in the county jail, we'd be held for murder, and with Runyan's and Toll's weight thrown against us we'd hang. I hadn't seen Ed Veach in the crowd. Now I squeezed my eyes shut, and when I opened them, I felt better. Veach, a huge hulk of a man, was standing over Mort's body, with his shirttail hanging over his pants and his gun belt buckled under the bulge of his belly. He was arguing with someone, one great fist pounding the air, and I heard him say, 'By God, it looks like murder to me.'

'We'd better get over there,' my father said. 'Feel better?'

'Yeah, I'm all right,' I said.

We holstered our guns, and walked across the street, our feet kicking up a cloud of dust. Sammy Blue was gone; he was probably in Doc Holt's office getting his arm set. Runyan was not in sight.

'Why do you call it murder, Ed?' my father asked.

Veach's big body heaved around. He looked at my father, his cheeks quivering. Usually they were round as if he were ready to blow out a great gust of air, but now they were droopy. He needed a shave, he was dirty, and his shirt sagged open where it had come unbuttoned showing his filthy under-shirt. For a moment his little eyes were pinned on my father's face. He tried to keep them there, but he failed. He was soft lard set against the hard bone and muscle of my father.

'Killing's murder, ain't it, Munro?' Veach said, staring at the ground.

'You're smarter'n that,' my father said. 'You know what Sammy Blue aimed to do. Did you expect us to stand there and get plugged like fish in a barrel?'

'How did you know what they were going to do?' Veach asked, still looking at the ground. 'You were walking the other way. You pulled your gun before you turned.'

'I know Sammy Blue,' my father said. 'I knew him a long time before I came to this country.'

Brown, the hotel clerk, was puffing up like an infuriated bullfrog. 'Damn it, Ed ...' he began.

'Knowing Blue don't change nothing,' Veach said stubbornly. 'You pulled your gun before you turned.'

'Did you see it?' my father asked.

'No, but I talked—'

'You got it wrong. We pulled our guns as we turned, not before. There's a hell of a lot of difference, Sheriff.'

Brown wouldn't be overlooked any longer. He grabbed Veach's arm and shook it. 'You listen to me, Ed. I saw what happened in the hotel lobby. Blue was pushing them; he wasn't going to let Munro here see Runyan. Tried to start a fight. He would have if I hadn't stopped him with a scatter-gun.'

'That's got nothing to do—' Veach began.

'Oh, for God's sake!' Brown said in disgust. 'Are you beholden to the Rafter 3? Or are you scared of Vic Toll?'

'I don't cotton to that kind of talk,' Veach said sullenly.

'You're gonna hear more of it if you don't get some sense into that fat skull of your'n,' Brown said. 'You arrest 'em for murder, and I'll tell in court what I just told you. When Mort came down the stairs, Blue says, "Let's get 'em." Them's his exact words. That's what I'll tell in court, Ed, and I'll swear you right out from under your star, and don't you forget it.'

I had a feeling Sammy Blue had been throwing his weight around town and no one liked it—no one except Ed Veach, anyhow. Maybe Veach didn't like it, either, but with Cameron Runyan in town he was doing his tightrope walking act again.

I don't know what would have happened if Brown hadn't spoken his piece. None of us who lived in the park were particularly popular in town. We were largely self-sufficient, we were so far away that we never came to Buhl unless it was absolutely necessary, and some of the park people preferred to make the longer trip to Rock Springs in Wyoming because it was on the railroad and bulky items like farm machinery and stoves and such were cheaper there.

On the other hand, a lot of people in the county were bitter because of the brutal and high-handed tactics Vic Toll used. It may have been that bitterness, or perhaps because Brown took the lead; but whatever the cause was, we suddenly were sided by half the men in the crowd.

Buffalo Bones Jester said, 'I seen it from the Belle Union, Sheriff. It ain't murder when a man defends himself.'

And the teacher, Rutherford Cartwright, 'That's right, Ed. I just turned the corner when it started. Self-defense. You can't call it anything else.'

Scissors McGuire, the barber, still wearing his apron, nodded. 'Just put me on the jury, Ed. I'd get the Munros acquitted so fast it'd make your head swim.'

Veach, red in the face and angry, sputtered: 'What's the matter with you boys? You was singing a different tune awhile ago.'

'We got to thinking,' Alec Brady said. He was the store-keeper and mayor, and one of the most respected men in Buhl. 'Runyan's been in town spring and fall every year since I came here, but this is the first time he ever brought a gunslick like Sammy Blue. We've eaten his dirt, Ed, you and me and all of us. Why? Because we were scared, that's why. If we're men, it's time we acted like it. We'd be a hell of a lot less than men if we let you arrest the Munros for a murder that wasn't murder at all.'

Reluctantly Veach said, 'Looks like I can't hold you, Munro. I'm gonna go see how Sammy Blue is.'

He walked away, moving slowly and ponderously. My father said, 'Thanks, boys.'

'No thanks necessary,' Brady said. 'I've just got one regret. I wish you'd killed Blue instead of breaking his arm. I hope to hell you hang onto the park, too.'

'We aim to,' my father said.

He turned and started toward the store. I fell into step beside him, saying, 'I don't feel like eating anything.'

'We'll get a drink first,' he said.

We went into the Belle Union. When I was alone, or with Gil or a neighbor, I asked for beer, or once in a while whiskey, but on the few occasions I had been here with my father, he had always ordered for me. Soda pop every time, but today he said, 'Whiskey.' Then he looked at me, smiling a little. 'You did a man's job today. Want a man's drink?'

'Whiskey,' I said, but I didn't feel like a man. I'd be a long time forgetting how Mort went down with the blood spurting out of the hole in his neck. I was glad I hadn't killed Sammy Blue, although I knew how my father felt. Many times I had heard him say: 'A gun is the last resort. Never use it unless you aim to kill the man you're drawing on.' He was right. A gunslick like Blue had a touchy pride, and someday I'd probably have to kill him or be

41

killed. Still, I was glad it hadn't happened today.

CHAPTER SIX

I slept until noon, and then I lay in bed awhile, thinking about what had happened in town, and about my father. I had done a man's work for years, but somehow I had never felt that my father accepted me as a man. Now I knew he did. Another thought occurred to me, and it bothered me a little. I had underestimated my father.

The fact that a sparrow of a woman like Ma had been able to dictate to my father was beyond my understanding, so I had assumed that he was weak. Or something. I don't really know what I assumed, but I did know he had never attained the stature in my eyes he should. The only time he had stood up to my mother was when he'd bought the Big Ten.

I remembered how he'd faced Sammy Blue in the hotel lobby, how he'd talked to Cameron Runyan in the cowman's hotel room, and how he'd handled the fight in the street, proof enough that he could have been a lawman and a good one. He had both gun savvy and guts, and something else that was an intangible, but an important one. I suppose you'd call it a knowledge of human nature, a quality a good lawman had to have. And all the time I'd thought he just didn't have what it took.

My mother pounded on the door. 'Dinner's ready, Dave,' she said.

'Coming,' I said, and got up and began to dress.

I had told my father I was pulling out, but now I knew I wouldn't. He was going to need me before the winter was over. Gil, for all of his gun skill, wouldn't do. My father knew that, or he'd have taken Gil with him yesterday.

And there was Kitsy. I'd marry her and bring her here, if she'd come. We'd have it rough in more ways than one. We might have to build a lean-to, or another cabin; my father couldn't afford to pay me any big wages. It would be a hell of a thing, Kitsy trying to get along with my mother. But we could try. I'd go over and see her after dinner. I'd see Bess, too, although I'd just about as soon face Sammy Blue again if he had a good right arm.

Gil didn't eat with us. 'He's over at Nordine's,' my mother said.

'Why doesn't he move over there?' I asked, and my father laughed.

'He would if he could,' he said.

As soon as I finished eating, I went outside and saddled up. I waited until my father left the house. I said, 'I'm not leaving.'

He smiled. 'I thought you wouldn't—or maybe I was just hoping.' I mounted and he added, 'Tell Bess what happened in town. I

43

didn't tell Gil.'

When I rode into the Anchor yard, I saw Gil sitting in a rocking chair on the porch, his feet cocked on the railing in front of him, smoking a cigar as if he didn't have a care in the world. I didn't want to see him again. I felt it so keenly that I veered off toward a shed beside the barn where Barney Lux was shoeing a horse.

Lux didn't bother to look at me when I reined up and dismounted. I said, 'Howdy, Barney.'

He said, 'Howdy,' and kept right on. He was a big sour man who never used two words if one would do, or none if a monosyllabic grunt would fill the bill. I don't know how long he'd worked for Bess, but he was here when we came. Bess was the only one who liked him. I think that was because he was satisfied with the wages she paid him, and he was the best cowhand in the park. He wasn't over thirty, maybe not that, and I often wondered why he stayed here when he could do a lot better working for Vic Toll.

Short Quinn, Bess's other rider, came out of the barn. He called, 'Don't you Munro boys have nothing to do but come over here and spark the Nordine girls?'

'Can you think of anything better to do?' I asked.

Shorty was about ten years older than Lux, and as different from him as day is from night. Kitsy was fond of him. He'd worked for the

Nordines as long as Kitsy could remember. 'Used to bounce me on his knee when I was little,' she told me, 'and when he went to town he always brought me some licorice candy. It made Bess mad because I got black all over my teeth and face.'

With Shorty, there was no mystery about why he stayed. He was bound to Anchor with the loyalty that is characteristic of cowboys. He played the mouth harp, he liked to sing. He'd go to town about once a month and turn his wolf loose, and Ed Veach would throw him into the cooler every time. When we had a dance or basket social at the schoolhouse, or our annual Thanksgiving turkey shoot, he had more fun than anyone else in the park. As far as I could see, Barney Lux never had any fun, and I doubted that he felt any loyalty to either Anchor or Bess.

'No, sir,' Shorty said. 'I can't think of nothing better than shining up to our girls.' He prodded the air with a forefinger in Gil's direction. 'But Bess can do a hell of a lot better'n that dude.'

Lux tossed his hammer into a corner of the shed. 'You know what's the matter with you hombres?'

'No,' I said. 'I'm happier not knowing what's the matter with me.'

'So'm I,' Shorty said. 'You got to take me the way I am, Barney. I'm too old to change.'

'I'll tell you anyway,' Lux said. 'You're

jealous. Alongside a purty boy like Gil, you look plumb ugly.' For some reason he thought that was funny. He led the horse out of the shed, laughing so hard his shoulders shook.

When he was gone, I said, 'Must be hell, working with that booger.'

'Ain't fun,' Shorty admitted.

I said: 'If I had to choose, I'd take Gil. Well, guess I'll see if Kitsy's in the house.'

'She's there,' Shorty said.

I tied my horse in front of the house and walked up the path. The Nordine ranch was the oldest one in the park, and Bess's and Kitsy's folks had been among the earliest settlers. At the time there wasn't even a doctor in Buhl. They'd had it rough in those days, I thought.

Bess was sitting beside Gil when I came up. She said, 'How are you, Dave? You haven't been over here for weeks.'

'That's why I'm here today,' I said. 'Didn't want to neglect you any longer.'

Gil snorted derisively. 'You letting on it's Bess you want to see?'

'She could do with a man around,' I said.

It didn't ruffle him much. He said, 'You won't fill the bill, kid. I see you decided to get out of bed.'

'I got hungry,' I said. 'I see you decided to fix the gate.'

He got red in the face then. He glanced at Bess, then he said, 'Ma allowed I'd better.'

I sat down on the porch and leaned against a post. 'Where's Kitsy?'

'Baking a cake,' Bess said.

'Maybe she'd like to see you,' Gil said. 'She don't have good judgment, but it'll come with age.'

I rolled a smoke. I was getting a little hot under the collar, but I didn't want to get into a ruckus with Gil over here. Bess was looking at me, a little amused, I thought, as if she considered me a kid, too.

She was twenty-five years old, but she looked older. A trace of gray showed in her dark brown hair. She was a big woman, about five eight, with good legs and ankles, and strong arms that could wrestle a calf at a branding fire almost as well as a man. She was a fine rider and could shoot with the best, and she knew the cattle business from A to Z.

In spite of her size, Bess was a good-looking woman, although she would have been the last to admit it. She seldom paid any attention to her hair. She brushed it and pinned it up and that was the end of it. If she had a tear in a sleeve or lost a button, she'd go right on wearing the dress until Kitsy fixed it.

She liked men. I think she preferred them to women, but the astonishing thing to me wasn't the fact that men liked her, but that they'd follow her. If she'd said we were going to raid the Rafter 3 and burn the buildings, she'd have had every man in the park riding with her except Elder Smith.

We were silent awhile, Gil wanting me to get out of there and Bess not caring much. At least I don't think she did. Finally I said, 'Pa and me had some trouble yesterday. He wanted me to tell you about it.'

'I'm listening,' Bess said.

'We went to town to see Cameron Runyan,' I said. 'Pa thought he could make Runyan see the light.'

'I told him he'd waste his time,' Bess said. 'I know that old booger.'

I told her how it had gone. Suddenly Gil got interested. He took his feet off the railing and leaned forward, and when I mentioned Sammy Blue, he said, 'I've heard of that hombre. A real gunslinger. I wish I'd gone with you.'

When I told about our fight, Gil shook his head, not believing a word of it. 'What kind of tobacco are you smoking, kid? You'd be flat on a table in Doc Holt's back room if you'd swapped lead with Sammy Blue.'

'I don't care if you believe it or not,' I said. 'I'm telling Bess. Pa figures we'll have trouble sure now.'

Bess had been listening closely. Now she said, 'It was coming, Dave. I figured it was better to show we had a little starch in our backbones than to sit here and let 'em throw five thousand head into the park.' She stood up, looking across the flat to the great wind-polished wall of rock on the other side of the

Big Red. 'Gil, you get on your horse and tell everybody we're having a meeting tonight in the schoolhouse.'

He didn't like it. A cold wind had come up, driving clouds in from the west. We hadn't had a real snow, but it felt as if one was on the way. I knew he'd rather sit right there in his rocking chair than make the long ride to the other end of the park. If Pa had asked, he'd have said he had a bellyache or something, but he never took that way out with Bess.

'All right,' he said, and got up.

'I'm going to see Elder Smith,' I said. 'You don't need to stop there.'

He was relieved. He didn't like Elder Smith, mostly because the old man saw through him. Gil had a talent for making people think he was something different from what he was, but Elder Smith had just as much talent for stripping the pretense off a man.

'Thanks, kid,' Gil said. 'I'll go right on from Frank Dance's place.'

I waited until he was gone, then I said, 'I've been wanting to talk to you, Bess.'

She had been friendly right up to that moment. Now her face was rigid, and her mouth, usually friendly and smiling, was a tight line across her teeth. 'Don't, Dave,' she said. 'I like you. Don't make me change.'

'I don't want you to change,' I said, 'but you keep treating me and Kitsy like we were kids— the way Gil does.'

'You are,' she said, 'but that's not the point. You know what my plans are for Kitsy.'

I got up and faced her. 'Bess, Pa said we could get married and live on the Big Ten. I can build a lean-to back of the house, or a cabin if that's what Kitsy wants. I was going to pull out, but I can't, with things stacking up the way they are. I can't live here, either, feeling the way I do about Kitsy and her feeling the way she does about me.'

'All right, Dave,' she said. 'I don't want to hear any more about it.'

As I stood there, open-mouthed, hurt, and angrier than I cared to admit, the ranch-house door was quietly, but effectively, shut in my face.

CHAPTER SEVEN

During our drifting years we had seen almost all of Colorado: the eastern plains, the high country, the big parks such as the San Luis Valley and South Park, the river valleys, the Arkansas and the Uncompahgre and the Grand, but to me there was no other place in the state that came close to Dillon's Park.

I thought about it now as I followed the lane from the Nordine place to the county road that paralleled the river. I had to get my mind off Kitsy, and Bess who stood between us, or I'd have gone crazy. I turned north toward Elder Smith's store, and rode along the fringe of willows that bordered the Big Red just to my left.

I rode past Frank Dance's Diamond 8, set at the base of Campbell Mountain. The rest of the ranches in the park were on the other side of Elder Smith's store, stretching out better than ten miles. Gil would have a ride before he got back, I thought. He'd be so tired when he got home he wouldn't come to the meeting.

The wind made a steady pressure against my face, and now I saw a few snowflakes in the air. Then, perhaps because it was cold, I got to thinking how it was in the park in the summertime, the days scorching hot, the nights just right. When the willows were leafed out, they made an impenetrable screen along the banks of the river.

Before Bess realized Kitsy and I were serious about each other, we used to sneak off and go swimming, usually after dark. Kitsy had always been able to ride anywhere at anytime, so Bess didn't think much about it when Kitsy took off after supper and didn't get back until ten or later.

The fact that neither one of us had a swimming suit didn't bother. Rather, it added something. I don't think modesty was involved. We just didn't have any inhibitions. There was a big rock at the edge of the pool, the water twenty feet deep below it. I'll never forget watching Kitsy climb to the top of that rock and dive off, something I was afraid to do. She had all the grace and perfection of a native trout in a high-country mountain stream; she'd hit the water like a thrown knife.

Sooner or later we were bound to be discovered, and it was our good luck it was Shorty Quinn who did the discovering. He was riding back from the store one night and heard us splashing around. He reined up and hollered. He wasn't over thirty feet away on the other side of the willows. We couldn't possibly get to our clothes in time, so Kitsy worked in close to the rock and stayed there, just her head showing, and I called to Shorty.

He got off his horse and came through the willows as I swam to the bank and crawled out. He asked, 'How's the water?'

I said, 'Perfect.' He squatted down a few feet from me and rolled a smoke. He didn't say a word about Kitsy, but her clothes were on a rock beside mine. I was scared, plenty scared.

Presently he said, 'You play with dynamite long enough and you'll get your head blown off.' He flipped his cigarette into the water and went on, 'What'll your Ma say when she hears? And Bess?'

He got up and went back through the willows. A moment later we heard him ride away. That was the last time we went swimming together. We could laugh about it now, but we were a pair of scared kids that night. Ma would have gone on for days about how indecent a thing like that was, and Kitsy said Bess would have taken a strap to her bare backside. She had often enough.

Now a sense of rebellion rose in me. They were all against us. Bess's attitude didn't make any sense. She was a stubborn woman, and once her mind was made up, that was the end of it. She'd dictate Kitsy's future even if it meant a break between them.

I was boiling inside when I reached the store, but I couldn't stay that way around Elder Smith. He called, 'Come on in, David. I'm glad to see you.' As I stepped down, he said, 'You look as if you've been consorting with a rattlesnake. What's biting you?'

'Nothing different than usual,' I answered.

'Put your horse in the shed,' he said. 'I've got a pot of mulligan on the stove. It'll be ready to eat before long.'

I put my horse in the shed behind the schoolhouse, next to the store. When I returned, he opened the door, calling out in his cheerful way, 'Come in.' He lived in this single room behind the store. The kitchen was on one side with a range and shelves that were filled with canned goods and sacks of food and dishes. A table and two rawhide-bottom chairs were in the middle of the room, and a bed was on the other side, with a rocking chair beside it.

The gossips in the valley claimed he had money buried under the floor. That may or may not have been true, but one thing was sure: he was an old man who lived an austere life and he'd go on living it as long as he was alive.

He closed the door behind me, motioned toward the rocking chair, and said, 'You tell me what's bothering you while I set the table.'

'You heard about driving the Rafter 3 cows out of the park and Bess shooting one of Toll's riders?' I asked. He nodded, and I went on. 'Well, you don't know what happened in town yesterday.' I told him, and all the time I was thinking about him.

*   *   *

I went to school to Elder Smith the first winter I was in the valley. Kitsy went, too. We rode together from the mouth of the Nordine lane to school and back in the evening, and that was when we fell in love with each other. As Kitsy said in the haymow the other day, we knew, even then.

Frank Dance's oldest boy Kip made a remark about Kitsy and me. He liked her too, I guess, and resented me, a newcomer, moving in and taking over. He was six months older than I was, and considerably heavier, but I licked hell out of him. After fighting Gil most of my life, I knew just about every trick in the book.

Elder Smith got us together the next day. I don't remember what he said, but after that Kip and I became good friends. I'm sure that if

54

Elder Smith hadn't taken a hand, we'd have been enemies and had real trouble before now. That was typical of him. Today the park was a tightly knit little community that would stand together against Rafter 3, and Elder Smith was responsible.

He was a tall thin man, a little stooped, and frail looking, but I don't think he was frail at all, except for the natural frailty of age. He must have been seventy, so he didn't do much work, but he gardened, kept a few chickens, a pig, and a cow, and he chopped his own wood.

He had an extraordinary ability for reading people.

We hadn't been in the park six months before he knew how it was between my father and mother, and he had Gil sized up right down to a gnat's eyebrow. I sensed that by talking to him, although he never came right out and said so. Sometimes I got the jitters thinking about it. He had me sized up, too, and I had a hunch I wouldn't like what he saw, if I knew what it was.

*   *   *

By the time I finished talking, he had the table set and had poured the coffee and filled our bowls with stew.

He motioned me to the table and said grace. After we began to eat, he said, 'You're lucky to be alive. I've heard of Sammy Blue.'

55

He got up presently and filled our bowls again, then sat down and pushed the dish of crackers at me. 'There is an image of God in every man, and we should try to see it, but with men like Runyan and Vic Toll it's hard to do. We have to try to understand them, and usually we can. Runyan was a poor man to start with. I knew him years ago in Wyoming when he was just a little rancher. We had hard times and a bank closed him out. After that, nothing could stop him. Seven years after he was bankrupt, he bought the bank and fired everyone who had been working there. In his mind all men are his enemies except those who work for him.'

He stirred his mulligan, frowning at it. 'I don't know anything about Toll when he was younger, but from what he's done since he started working for Runyan I'd say he had a hard childhood. He doesn't understand love and probably doesn't even admit its existence. All of us have our satisfactions in one way or another, David. His way is to make people afraid of him. We pull him down or he pulls us down.'

'Pa says people are afraid of him,' I agreed. 'Not Runyan or gunslingers like Sammy Blue. Pa says he's grown into a legend.'

'That's true. He's set on having Dillon's Park for Rafter 3 winter range. He'll get it or he'll die trying. Runyan could never find another man like him.'

He was silent until he finished his stew, then sat back and looked at me. 'This wasn't what was bothering you, David.'

'No,' I said. 'Bess is calling a meeting for tonight at the schoolhouse.'

He nodded, unwilling to be sidetracked. 'Now what was it that you were fretting about?'

I didn't want to talk about it, but when I looked at Elder Smith's face I saw understanding there, and I had a haunting feeling he knew before I ever said a word. Suddenly I wanted to talk, and I did. I told him I'd gone over to Nordine's and Bess wouldn't even listen. When I finished I felt better just for the telling, as if the pressure that had been gathering inside me had been relieved.

He nodded, and I had a warm feeling that he sympathized with me. He said: 'Plato tells us that self-conquest is the greatest of all victories. You haven't quite achieved it yet, David, but you will. Your trouble is you're young and youth has no talent for waiting. But that's what you've got to do. You can't run off and leave your father, even though you've felt like it at times. You can't take Kitsy, either. She's all Bess has, just as you're all your father has. I know you won't find any comfort in this, David, but time will bring a solution. Believe me, I know. If you precipitate action, you'll provoke tragedy. The seeds of it are already here.' He motioned eastward in the direction of the Rafter 3. 'Don't plant any more, whatever you do.'

He was right. But, as he admitted, there was no comfort in the thought of waiting for time to solve a problem like this.

I was thinking about what he had said when I heard someone call, 'Hello!' Elder Smith got up and walked to the window. When he turned, his face was more grim than I had ever seen it before. He said, 'Vic Toll is outside.'

CHAPTER EIGHT

I followed Elder Smith through the door, not having the slightest idea why Vic Toll was here in the park. I wasn't wearing my gun. At first I wished I had it, then I was glad I didn't. I couldn't expect to match Vic Toll if it came to a gun fight, and as long as I wasn't armed he couldn't prod me into making a try.

'Step down and come in, Mr. Toll,' Elder Smith said. 'We just finished eating, but there's plenty more...'

'No, thanks.' Toll gave me a sharp look, and asked, 'Ain't you the Munro kid?'

'I'm Dave Munro,' I said.

He sat with a hand on the saddle horn, staring at me in the dusk light. He seemed even bigger than he'd been the time I saw him in the Belle Union more than three years ago. His face was darker, his chin a little more over-grown, his nose a little more hooked. More overbearing, too, I thought, and more dangerous.

I remembered my father saying Toll had become a legend. He was brutal and ruthless enough, certainly, and the tales of his brutality and ruthlessness had spread all over the county, as well as here in the park, but another man could have been as bad as Toll and never have achieved his reputation. He looked the part. That, I felt, was the answer. Staring at him now, a few fat snowflakes drifting between us, I had a feeling he was as unchangeable as the great rock cliff on the other side of the Big Red.

'You shot Sammy Blue the other day,' he said.

'That's right.'

'I was just fixing to tell you that his right arm will be good as ever. Don't make much difference, anyhow. He's as good with his left as his right. You'd better light a shuck out of the country, kid. No man's luck runs good twice in a row with Sammy Blue.'

Toll's eyes turned to Smith. 'You're the man I came to see. You'll be having a meeting before long, I reckon.'

'Tonight,' Elder Smith said.

'I figured so,' Toll said. 'You tell 'em we don't want trouble no more'n you park folks do, but we've always wintered a few head in the park and nobody's kicked. We don't see no reason for you people to kick now.'

'I'll tell them,' Elder Smith said.

'And tell them something else. We don't like to have our cows run to hell an' gone, and I don't want my men shot. One of 'em is flat on his back and he'll be that way for a month or more.'

'All right,' the Elder said.

'Now here's something you don't need to tell 'em.' From the tone of Toll's voice, I had a feeling this was what he had really come to say. 'You're a leader, ain't you, Smith? They do about what you say, don't they?'

'Not always,' Elder Smith answered.

'Often enough for you to pay attention to what I'm saying. You be damned sure you lead 'em the right way. Something might happen to you if you don't, you and anybody else hereabouts who figures he's a leader.'

'You're threatening murder,' Smith said. 'That it?'

'Call it whatever you want to,' Toll said. 'Just remember, there was a man who was making big medicine a few years ago. He had a little trouble.'

'A bullet in his back,' Elder Smith said. 'His name was Herb Jason.'

'Yeah, I believe it was,' Toll said, and without another word, he whirled his horse and disappeared in the dusk.

We went back inside and Elder Smith built

up the fire. He looked at me, and I saw the trouble that was in his face. He said: 'Toll could bring his men and clear us all out of the valley, burn our houses and kill us, but if he did that the sheriff would have to do something. Newspapers all over the country would carry headlines about a massacre. He doesn't want that kind of publicity, so he won't handle it that way.'

He carried the dirty dishes to the back of the stove, then turned to me again. 'Herb Jason was a loudmouth. He did some talking in town about how Cameron Runyan got his start with a running iron and how they were still using the same tactics. Frank Dance found him on the east slope of Campbell Mountain, shot in the back with a .30–.30.'

'But we don't have any loudmouths now,' I said.

'No, but we have Bess, who's the real leader in the park,' he said. 'Far more of a leader than she was three years ago when Herb got it. We have your father, who killed Runyan's man in town. We've driven Rafter 3 cows out of the park, and a Rafter 3 man was shot.'

He turned back to the stove, filled a dishpan with hot water, and began washing dishes. I knew what he meant. Toll would pick off the leaders just as he'd picked off Herb Jason. The sheriff would say he couldn't find the killer. And what would happen after a murder or two? Our resistance would collapse.

'Go over to the schoolhouse and build a fire,' Elder Smith said. 'I'll be over in a minute.'

He wanted to do some thinking, I suppose. I wondered what I'd do if my life had been threatened. Elder Smith was an old man, but he had no more desire to die than I did. Still, I knew what he'd say.

I built a fire in the potbellied stove in the middle of the schoolhouse, then wandered around, looking at the desk where I had carved my initials the winter I was in school. A lot of memories here, I thought as I walked around the room. Even for me, and I had been in school only the one winter. Kitsy had gone through the grades here. So had Kip Dance and a lot of others. Every family but ours had lived here a generation. Homes were filled with memories, too, many more than the schoolhouse, or the church across the road, sweet and bitter and poignant ones, all kinds of memories that come from people living together, living and dying, loving and hating. Now we faced murder, and we might just as well admit it.

People began drifting in after that, stomping snow off their feet at the door and grumbling a little about the weather. Frank Dance and his son Kip, Luke Jordan, Matt Colohan, Johnny Strong, who lived at the other end of the park and had had the longest ride and didn't grumble at all, then my father and Gil, who looked tired.

They were all there except Bess when Elder Smith came in a little before eight. He went directly to my father and talked to him in low tones. He had said he'd be over in a minute, but it had been considerably more than an hour. He looked old and very tired.

At five minutes after eight Bess had not showed up. Elder Smith looked at his watch, then called to Gil, 'Bess was going to be here, wasn't she?'

'Sure she was,' Gil said. 'She had important business to bring up.'

Elder Smith fidgeted for a minute or so, said something to my father.

Frank Dance called, 'Let's get started, Elder.'

'Looks like we'd better,' Elder Smith agreed.

He walked to the front of the room and, going behind his desk, picked up a gavel. We had no regular schedule of meetings. They were called just as this one had been tonight, but with that exception our meetings were formal. Elder Smith insisted on order and had the minutes carefully kept and read. But Bess was the secretary, and she had the minutes of the last meeting.

Elder Smith raised the gavel, then lowered it. Bess's absence apparently disturbed him. I'd been to all the meetings since we moved to the park, and this was the first time Bess hadn't been here. Smith laid the gavel down, opened a drawer and, taking out a tablet and pencil, handed them to Kip Dance who sat in the front row beside his father.

'You keep the minutes until Bess gets here,' Smith said.

'Nobody can read my writing,' Kip said.

'You can,' the Elder said.

He picked up the gavel and raised it just as the door opened and Kitsy slipped into the room. We were all surprised, and shocked too, I think. We had expected Bess, but here was Kitsy, who had never, to my knowledge, been to a meeting.

Elder Smith lowered the gavel again. 'Is Bess coming?' he asked.

'I don't know,' Kitsy said. 'She was awful busy when I left home and I didn't get a chance to ask her. I came to tell you not to wait.'

Gil turned around to stare at Kitsy. He asked, 'What's Bess so busy about?'

'She's just ... busy,' Kitsy said, and dropped into the seat beside me.

Elder Smith pounded for order and announced that Kip Dance would keep the minutes in the absence of the secretary, but I wasn't listening. The instant I saw Kitsy, I realized she was excited about something, but I didn't have any idea what had happened until she leaned close to me and put her mouth against my ear.

'Vic Toll had supper at our place,' she said. 'After we finished, they went into the front room and shut the door and I did the dishes. I heard them arguing, real loud; then I didn't hear anything. Just before I came over here, I looked through the keyhole.'

She stopped and pulled her head back, wanting me to ask what she saw. Her eyes were about to pop out of her head. I still had no idea what had happened, then the thought struck me that Vic Toll had strangled Bess, or slit her throat, or something. But that was crazy.

I asked, 'Well?'

She put her mouth back to my ear again. 'He was kissing her!' she said triumphantly. 'But don't tell anybody. Bess would skin me alive if she knew I'd told.'

CHAPTER NINE

Bess came in a few minutes after Kitsy did. She marched up the aisle and sat down beside Kip Dance, laying the secretary's book on the desk in front of her. As usual, she had paid little attention to her appearance. She wore a black riding skirt and a leather jacket over a tan blouse. Her boots, wet with snow, hadn't been polished for weeks. She didn't even bother to take off her old Stetson. If she was upset in any way, she didn't show it.

Elder Smith was disturbed if Bess wasn't. He sounded irritated when he said, 'You called the meeting, Bess, and you're late.'

'I apologize,' Bess said.

Seated in the rear of the room, I could only see the back of her head; but, knowing Bess, I was convinced she was looking directly at him and not batting an eye. That was Bess Nordine for you. If she ran into a grizzly in her back yard, she'd stare him down and go right on about her business.

'We'll dispense with the minutes of the last meeting,' Elder Smith said, 'inasmuch as our secretary was late. Kip, you can let Bess keep the minutes for this meeting, now that she's here.'

Plainly relieved, Kip shoved the paper and pencil on his side of the desk toward Bess. She took it, smiling, and whispered something to him. I wondered what would happen if Kitsy got up and said, 'When I left home, Bess was kissing Vic Toll.' I almost laughed out loud. Shooting a gun off in the middle of the meeting wouldn't have kicked up any more commotion.

Elder Smith blew out a long breath, his mustache fluttering. He said, 'Bess, will you state your reason for calling the meeting?'

'I'll be glad to, Elder,' Bess said, and got up and faced the room.

She told about driving Rafter 3 cows out of the park and shooting one of the Rafter 3 riders. She went on, 'I offer no apologies. There were two of them. I thought they were going to pull their guns, so I fired. Vic Toll had supper with us tonight. He says his man will be in bed for a month or more. I say I'm not sorry. He was helping drive Rafter 3 cattle into the park. Toll admits it was a test. If we'd let them stay, we'd have five thousand head in here by Thanksgiving.'

Bess was a good speaker, talking clearly and smoothly, with none of the hesitation and throat clearing that bothered the rest of us. Every man in the room must have known what the action meant, but I doubt that anyone condemned her.

'We might just as well face facts,' she said. 'Rafter 3 has more men than we have, and money to hire still more, which we don't have. Money to hire lawyers, too, if we're dragged into court. On the face of it, it looks like we're whipped before we start, but I say we're not. We know we've got barely enough grass in the park to get our stock through the winter. If we allow Rafter 3 to steal our grass, we will be whipped.'

She sat down. She had more to say, I thought, but she was smart enough not to hog the show. She knew exactly how far she could go at any given time, and how fast she could travel.

Elder Smith nodded at my father. 'Joe, tell what happened in town.'

My father rose and told what had happened, emphasizing that Runyan had refused to take any responsibility for Toll's actions.

The men looked at my father with new respect, all but Gil, and some of them turned around and looked at me. Kitsy squeezed my hand and I stared at the top of the pencil-scarred desk, my face red.

Elder Smith nodded at Bess. 'Did Toll indicate to you what he planned to do?'

'No,' Bess answered. 'He just said Runyan's patience was worn out, and that the smart thing for us to do was to sell.' She turned so she could see everyone in the room. 'Gentlemen, I for one will never sell to Cameron Runyan.'

'None of us will,' Elder Smith said. 'I'm an old man, and perhaps I shouldn't speak for the rest of you who are younger and have more of your life to live than I have, but for me it is better to die than to surrender. The history of mankind is the story of men like Cameron Runyan forcing injustice upon weaker men. The only chance we have of making progress toward a better world is to fight injustice wherever we find it. Our fighting it here in our small way is a part of the big fight that goes on constantly all over the world.'

Frank Dance said, 'We're not going to sell, Elder. I'll kill the first man who does. But what are we going to do?'

Elder Smith nodded at Bess. 'Do you have a notion about what we should do?'

'Yes, I do,' she said, and, standing up, faced us again. 'The Mormons west of us won't give us any trouble. South we've got the canyon of

68

the Big Red. Nobody's coming from that direction. That leaves us wide open on the north and east. Fencing is no good. Too slow and too expensive. Besides, Toll would cut it. We don't have enough men to ride the boundary. There is only one practical thing we can do. It'll go against your prejudices, but give it some thought before you jump the gun.'

She hesitated, glancing at Elder Smith, at my father, finally at Frank Dance, then she plunged on: 'For years we've kept sheep out of the park. Now it's time to change our policy. Inside of a week we can have a couple of bands from Utah in here. Put one on the other side of Campbell Mountain, the second just this side of Buck Creek, and we'll have a wall all around the park. Rafter 3 cattle won't cross it.'

For once she lost a little of her self-confidence. She must have sensed the storm of disapproval that her suggestion was bound to meet, but she wasn't to be stopped at this point. She faced Elder Smith. 'I move we contact two sheepmen at once and invite them here.'

As she sat down, Gil called, 'I second the motion.'

She had him cocked and primed, I thought. I doubted that anyone else would have seconded her motion.

Frank Dance jumped up. 'Mr. Chairman, we'd be loco to take one poison to get rid of another!'

Johnny Strong was on his feet before Dance

was down. 'Mr. Chairman, this is more than prejudice. It's suicide. We'd have sheep all over the park in a year. Our range would be shot to hell.'

And Matt Colohan, 'I say the same. Open the gates to one damned woolly and they'll pour in.'

Luke Jordan was up, so angry he was trembling. He said, 'Mr. Chairman.' He swallowed, the corners of his mouth working. He pulled a bandanna out of his pocket and wiped his face. 'Mr. Chairman, I was in a cattle-sheep war, so I'm probably the only man in the park who knows what he's talking about. It's purty damned plain Bess don't. I'd rather lose everything we've got to Cameron Runyan than to let sheep into the park.'

Bess said nothing. She must have expected this. In any case, she did not make an issue of it. When my father called, 'Question,' Elder Smith said, 'Those in favor of the motion say aye.' Only Bess and Gil voted, but when he asked for those opposed, there was a shout. Elder Smith said, smiling faintly, 'The motion's lost.'

Gil got up. 'Mr. Chairman, I helped drive that bunch of Rafter 3 stuff off our range. My father and brother were almost murdered in Buhl. Our Big Ten is the closest ranch to Rafter 3 range. We'd be the first to get hit, so maybe we've been thinking more about this than the rest of you have. Sheep might not be the answer, but we've got to find one. The way I see it, if Toll lost money on having his cattle in the park he'd be damned glad to keep 'em out.'

He stopped, looking around to see how the others were taking what he'd said. He swallowed and licked his lips. Scared, I thought. He'd never made a speech in his life to my knowledge, but Bess had him coached for this one. It was pretty plain to me what had happened. Bess had two plans. She didn't want to give both of them herself, so she'd persuaded Gil to present the other one.

'I say we've got to fight fire with fire,' Gil went on. 'Toll wants to steal our grass, so let's steal his cattle. A running iron can be as good a weapon as a shooting iron. It'd be easy enough to change a Rafter 3 to a Diamond 8, for instance. Come spring, we can brand any Rafter 3 calf we find on our range and get rid of the cow. A little of that and Toll will keep his stock out of the park.'

It was a bald proposal to go into a planned campaign of rustling. We might as well, I thought, talk about a stage holdup or robbing the bank in Buhl. Everyone sat in a kind of stunned silence after Gil sat down. Maybe Frank Dance had changed a few Rafter 3's into Diamond 8's. I don't know. I do know the park had the reputation of being a hangout for rustlers. Runyan had seen to that. Newspapers had printed some terrible stories about us. But for Gil to suggest in open meeting that we rustle Rafter 3 cattle as a means of striking back was something else.

There was a lot of shuffling around and whispering, and then Elder Smith said sadly, 'I'm surprised, Gil. You should realize that no man can erase one crime by committing another.'

'I don't figure that's the point,' Frank Dance said. 'Gil's talking sense when he says we've got to fight fire with fire.'

Johnny Strong said, 'It'll work, Frank. It'll work us right into the Canon City pen.'

'Not if we're careful,' Luke Jordan said.

Then my father. 'I won't have any part of this. If we've got to fight fire with fire, we'll use gunfire, not a branding fire.'

CHAPTER TEN

Snow seldom stayed on very long in the park, especially the early snows. That was true this time. By noon the next day it was gone. I had been helping my father cut our winter's supply of wood high up on a shoulder of Campbell Mountain, but there was no use to go back now. We'd be mired down in two feet of snow.

So we went to work sorting apples and putting away the root crops, a chore my mother would have done sooner or later. Except for the plowing and harrowing and

72

fertilizing in the spring, the garden was Ma's job, sometimes with a little help from Gil when she caught him right. This time Gil must have guessed what we were going to do because he went hunting.

We had several pear and apple trees in the yard. In between other jobs I had picked the pears and apples; Ma had canned the pears and we'd stored the apples in the root cellar. Now we had to sort the apples, putting the wormy, hail-pitted ones that were already beginning to spoil in one pile, the good apples that would last until late spring in another. We finished the job the day after the snow because we couldn't get on the garden, as wet as it was.

This was the kind of work I enjoyed, sitting beside my father in the gloom of the root cellar, Gil gone and my mother peeling and canning the culls in the kitchen. My father enjoyed it, too, I think. For the moment at least we shared a feeling of comradeship that was rich and complete.

We made small talk, avoiding the ugly topics that worried us: Gil's laziness and Bess's attitude toward me and Kitsy, and Rafter 3's greed. My father, I was sure, found the satisfaction here that he had looked forward to for so long. He even got around to telling me that, come spring, he was going to borrow money from the bank in Buhl to buy some good Shorthorn bulls. There would be no point of that unless he could persuade the other park ranchers to get rid of their grade bulls and invest in good stock.

'We could put two, three hundred more pounds on a steer if we had purebred bulls,' he said, 'but it's gonna be a hell of a job to make Luke Jordan and Matt Colohan see it. I've talked to a few of the boys. Johnny Strong's with me 100 per cent. Frank Dance and most of the others will go along, but Luke and Matt can't see it. I was figuring on bringing it up last night, but I saw that wasn't the time.'

Neither Kitsy nor Bess was in church Sunday morning. I wondered about it because they came regularly, and I couldn't remember a Sunday since I'd been in the park that both of them had missed.

I was the first one out of the building. Usually I lingered to visit the way everybody else did, and then I'd ride to the Nordine place with Kitsy, Bess and Gil just ahead of us or behind us. This time I didn't wait for Gil. I had a hunch something was wrong. Maybe Kitsy was sick.

But after worrying about it all the way from the church house to Anchor, I still didn't come up with anything that was as bad as the truth. While I was still in the lane, Barney Lux stepped out of the bunkhouse with his .30–.30. He waited for me in front of the house, the Winchester lined on my brisket.

'Don't get off that horse, sonny,' Lux said as if he enjoyed saying it. 'Just turn around and keep going. You ain't seeing Kitsy no more.'

I never had liked Lux. At that moment I liked him less than ever. I had a bad habit of putting everybody who did me dirt into a room and locking them up together: Gil, Bess, and Vic Toll especially. Now I shoved Lux into that room and turned the lock. I sat my saddle wanting to get off my horse and knock his teeth down his throat, but he looked mean with that rifle in his hand.

Finally I asked, 'Why?'

'Dunno. Bess just said you ain't coming around here no more.'

'Kitsy sick?'

'Hell, no.'

I didn't know what to do. I had a right to find out what this was about, but I didn't know how to get past that rifle. Lux wasn't gifted with patience. He said: 'Drag it, kid. By God, I mean it!'

I was ready to dig in my spurs and ride the bastard down when Shorty Quinn came around the house. He yelled: 'Hold it, Barney! I'll take care of this.'

Lux backed up, his eyes wicked. 'I don't need no help.'

'You shoot him and I'll blow your damned head off your shoulders,' Shorty said.

Shorty had his gun in his hand. I said, 'He means it, too, Barney.'

Lux kept backing off until he could see Shorty. He said sullenly, 'All right, you handle it.' He wheeled and stalked back to the bunkhouse.

Shorty dropped his gun into its holster and walked toward me, shaking his head. 'Sorry, Dave. That son of a bitch gets meaner all the time. Seems like Bess ain't much better lately. I sure can't figure her.'

'What's this about me not seeing Kitsy?'

'It's true. I don't know the whys and wherefores of it, but them's Bess's orders.'

'I've always been able to see Kitsy at church,' I said. 'What's happened now?'

He dug a toe through the dirt, still damp from the last snow. He knew something, I thought, but he wasn't sure he ought to tell me. I said: 'Shorty, you and me have always been good friends, and Kitsy thinks a lot of you. Now I aim to find out about this if I have to bust into the house—'

'Be hell to pay if you do,' he said. 'Well, I'll tell you what I know if you'll promise to go on home and behave yourself. Ain't nothing you can do but wait till Kitsy's eighteen, but if you get hurt trying to see her now, or hurt somebody else, you'll make things a lot worse.'

I knew then it was bad. I said, 'All right; I promise.'

'They had a fight,' Shorty said. 'A hell of a fight it must have been, too. A hair pulling, scratching, biting kind of a fight. Me'n Barney was out on the range, so we didn't see it. Let's see now. It was the day after you'd had that

76

meeting at the schoolhouse. I don't know what the ruckus was over, but when we got in that night they looked like they'd tangled with a painter. That was when Bess ordered us to keep you off the place. Next day Kitsy had a chance to talk to me. She said to tell you not to make trouble. She'd figure out a way to see you.'

I must have sat my saddle a full minute, just looking down at Shorty. He wouldn't lie, but I found this hard to believe. Finally I said, 'All right, Shorty. You let me know if Kitsy needs me.'

I rode off then. I could only guess what had happened. Kitsy must have made the mistake of telling Bess she knew about her and Vic Toll. Maybe she'd threatened to spread the story all over the park if Bess didn't let us get married. Hard to tell how far it had gone between them, as headstrong as they were.

Kitsy had told Shorty she'd figure out a way to see me. I wished she wouldn't, for a while at least. It would only lead to more and worse trouble.

CHAPTER ELEVEN

By Monday enough of the snow had gone off Campbell Mountain so that we were able to get back to our wood chopping. My father, his patience finally worn out, shook Gil awake before sunup. 'You're not going hunting today. We've got a winter's supply of wood to get off the mountain and we've got to do it before it snows again. Roll out now. You're going to help.'

He did, too. For once Ma didn't say a word. There were times, and this was one, when I thought she was seeing what she had done to Gil. A man can't go on mooching off his folks and his neighbors, and that was just about all Gil had ever done.

This time he fooled me. He stayed with us all week and didn't come up with a lame back or sore throat or one of the other dodges he'd used in the past. He didn't go over to see Bess in the evenings, either. Maybe he was too tired, but maybe there was another reason, too. If Bess really was interested in Vic Toll, she wouldn't have any time for Gil.

But how Bess felt about Gil was the least of my worries. I had Kitsy to think about. If the situation between her and Bess was as bad as Shorty Quinn had said, it couldn't go on. There was bound to be a blowup.

It started to rain on Saturday afternoon, just a mild drizzle, but by night we were thoroughly soaked. We changed our clothes when we got home, Pa milked, and when he came back into the house, Ma had a hot supper ready for us. I went to bed a few minutes later. A long day with a crosscut and a maul and wedge is enough to wear out any man.

My bedroom had been a small storeroom in the back of the house next to the kitchen. There were only two bedrooms in the house, and I didn't want to share one with Gil any more than he wanted to share one with me. I was content with my room, even though it was so small that I had less than two feet between my bed on one side and the bureau which was set against the other wall.

I think I went to sleep at once. Sometime during the night I was aware that the guinea hens were making a racket. Might be a coyote, I thought. They'd potrack at the drop of a hat or less. I thought sleepily I ought to get my gun out of the top drawer of the bureau and go out and see about it, but the bed was warm and it was wet and cold outside, so I just turned over.

The next thing I knew someone was tapping on my window. Scared, I rolled out of bed, yanked my bureau drawer open and fumbled around in the darkness for my gun, then I heard Kitsy's voice, 'Dave. Wake up, Dave.'

This was the last thing I expected. I got a match off the bureau, scratched it into life, and held the flame against the glass. It wasn't a dream. Kitsy was there, all right, her face pressed against the windowpane.

Startled by the match flame, she jumped back. I heard her muffled voice, 'Don't light a lamp. Come outside.'

'Soon as I dress.' I said.

I got into my shirt and pulled on my pants

and boots, all the time wondering what had happened to make her do this. She was standing beside the back door when I opened it. I said, 'Come in.'

'No, you come out,' she said. 'Your folks mustn't know anything about this.'

It was crazy, but I didn't want to argue. I grabbed my slicker and Stetson off a nail on the kitchen wall and went outside, shutting the door behind me. We crossed the yard to the barn, the mud sucking at our heels, the rain coming down harder than it had in the afternoon.

Kitsy didn't say a word; she just walked beside me, her hand on my arm. No moon, and with the clouds and the rain, the night was pit black. When we reached the barn I felt along the wall until we came to the door. We went in and I shut the door and lighted the lantern. Kitsy was in my arms at once, crying, 'Dave, Dave, I just can't get along without you.'

I kissed her, her arms hugging me with all her fierce young strength. When she drew her head back, I saw that she had been crying. Her face was wet with rain and tears. She looked thoroughly bedraggled and I mentally cursed Bess.

'I'm running away,' Kitsy said, 'and you've got to go with me. We'll get married in Buhl. We'll get jobs. We'll make out, Dave. I know we will.'

I was shocked because I had not expected it

to go this far, then I was scared. We'd talked about getting married. We'd dreamed our dreams and made our plans, but marriage had always been a distant thing, something in the future that we could do when our troubles were ironed out. Now it was right here, and I knew I wasn't ready for it.

'We'll talk about it tomorrow,' I said. 'I'll put your horse up and you come into the house. I'll have Ma fix a bed in the front room on the couch and—'

'No,' she cried. 'We're leaving. Now. You saddle your horse and get a few things you need. You can do it without waking your folks up. Leave them a note. We can get to Buhl by noon tomorrow and we'll get married.'

Her hands were gripping the front of my coat, her mouth a determined line. I said, 'We just can't jump into it like this. We haven't got any money...'

'Yes, we have,' she cut in. 'I took all there was in the house. Bess will say I stole it, but I've got a right to something. She can have the ranch.'

'How much have you got?'

She stared at the ground. 'Thirty-two dollars. But—but you have some, don't you?'

I laughed. There wasn't anything funny about this, but still I laughed. It was so crazy. 'Do you know how much I've got? Twelve dollars! How long do you think we could live on forty-four dollars? We'd have to come back home with our tails dragging. We can't do it, Kitsy. We've got to wait.'

'I'm done waiting,' she said. 'I've stood a lot off Bess. I won't stand any more. She won't let me see you. Not even at church. I can't go to the turkey shoot. No parties. No dances. I'm almost eighteen. She's bossed me around all my life, and I'm not going to stand it any longer.'

'What was your fight over?'

'I told her I saw her kissing Vic Toll and I said she was selling us out. I told her I knew she was going to marry Toll and then Rafter 3 would have the toe hold in the park they've wanted all this time. I said she'd sold her saddle, and then she got mad and hit me.'

'She didn't deny that she was going to marry Toll?'

'She didn't say anything. Just slapped me and I slapped her back. She said she was going to make me go to school in Denver. She wasn't going to have me marrying a—a pauper like you.'

That made me mad. Kitsy knew it would. Still, I shook my head. 'We can't get married now. There aren't any jobs in Buhl, winter coming on and all. Let's wait until spring—'

'Wait, wait, wait,' she screamed. 'I tell you I won't go on waiting. I love you, Dave. I don't want to waste any more time waiting.' She swallowed. 'Darling, I don't even want to live if it's got to be the way it has been the last few days.'

I stared at her, feeling absolutely helpless. I wasn't aware of anything else, I guess, or I would have heard the door open. Barney Lux said, 'You bastard! I told you to stay away from her.'

I whirled. Kitsy screamed. Lux was standing in the doorway, Bess behind him. I drove at Lux but I didn't reach him. He had a gun in his hand. He raised it and brought the barrel down in a hard blow that ripped past my left ear and struck me on the shoulder. I went down on my knees into the barn litter. The pain was so excruciating I couldn't hold back the groan that came through my tight lips. I thought my collarbone was broken.

Kitsy screamed again and lunged at Lux. He stepped aside and she stumbled past him. Bess caught her and held her. 'You've got to come home, Kitsy. I can't let you do this.'

I got on my feet and swung from my knees. The blow never landed. Lux hit me with his fist and knocked me down. 'That's enough, Barney,' Bess said. 'Come on. We've got what we came for.'

But Lux didn't move. He stood grinning down at me. Again I got up. I tried, but my blow was short. He knocked me down with his fist again, and after that it seemed to me I was paralyzed. I wasn't unconscious. I could see and hear, but I couldn't move. Bess said, 'Barney, I told you not to hit him again.'

Kitsy wasn't struggling any more. She was crying. Bess pulled her out of the doorway. That was the last I saw of her. After they were gone, Gil came in and helped me to my feet. 'I heard a racket out here,' he said. 'Thought I'd better see what it was.'

He was wet enough to have been standing in the rain for quite a while. He'd been afraid to interfere, I thought. He helped me into the house and got Ma up. He started a fire, and I undressed and fell into bed. Pa came into my room and examined my shoulder.

'You got a hell of a wallop,' he said, 'but I don't think it's broken.'

He went back into the kitchen, and I heard the three of them talking in low tones. I couldn't make out the words. Ma came in with a pan of hot water and a towel. She bathed my shoulder and the cuts on my face, then got some liniment and rubbed my shoulder. I thought she was going to burn my arm right off the body.

She rose, the lamp behind her throwing her shadow across my bed. 'I know it hurts, Dave. If you want me to bathe it again, or anything, you holler.'

They went to bed, and there was nothing I could do but tough it out.

The next morning Shorty Quinn came over. He said Bess and Kitsy had left for Denver.

CHAPTER TWELVE

Along with the Christmas program and the Fourth of July celebration, the Thanksgiving dinner and turkey shoot was one of the big annual events in the park. Elder Smith handled the whole business, even to raising the turkeys. A big tom was given for first prize, a hen for second. He made the targets and set them up, and arranged for someone to judge, usually a man from outside the park.

This year he asked Si Beam to do it. Beam was a little white-haired man, an itinerant peddler who visited the park every fall and spring. He didn't really compete with Elder Smith's store because the store carried only the essentials. Beam sold gimcracks of one sort or another, mostly to the women: bright cloth for dresses and aprons, needles, thread, Indian blankets, and even items like water pitchers, vases, and colored prints for the wall.

No one objected to Beam. He'd done the judging before, and was well known and liked. He always stayed with Bess when he came to the park. He'd stayed with her folks when they were alive, so he kept on, although several others, particularly Frank Dance, asked him to stay with them.

This year the turkey shoot started off the same as any other year. The crowd gathered behind the schoolhouse; the sky was clear, the air cold and crisp, holding the promise of winter. Snow still clung to the top of Campbell Mountain. Matt Colohan, the park whiskey maker, passed his jug around; there was the usual joshing and big talk, with each man bragging about how he'd knocked the bull's-eye out of the target, and Gil telling them they might as well save their powder because he could outshoot any man in the park.

But for me it was not like any other year simply because Kitsy wasn't there. Thanksgiving? Well, I had very little to be thankful for. I knew how she felt, too, living among strangers hundreds of miles away on the other side of the mountains. I'd had several letters from her, and not once had she indicated she was unhappy. She'd keep a stiff upper lip, I thought, because she didn't want to worry me, but I could read between the lines.

'I'm not coming home for Christmas,' she wrote. 'It's too long a trip to make just for a visit, so I won't see you until summer. Don't fret about me, Dave. It's sort of fun living with a bunch of girls. The food's good and everything is clean and nice. When I first got here, I thought I couldn't wait, but now I know I can. We'll get married next summer, Dave. I keep thinking of what Elder Smith has said so many times in his sermons, that everything works together for good for those who love God. You keep thinking that, too, Dave. It'll work out. I know it will.'

I wrote to her that I knew it would, too. I tried not to let her sense in my letters that I was filled with bitterness. I was afraid she would meet the kind of man Bess wanted her to marry, a lawyer or a doctor or someone who could give her luxuries I never could. I told myself I was doing Kitsy an injustice, that she would always love me and nothing could change her; but I realized now, better than ever before, how young we were, and then I would remember she'd be gone for many months and there was no telling how those months would change her.

Just before the shooting started, Bess came to me. Barney Lux wasn't in the crowd. He seemed to enjoy his own company better than anyone else's, and seldom came to any of the park gatherings. Still, I couldn't keep from saying to Bess: 'I see Barney isn't around. Maybe he was afraid I'd be here.'

'You know better, Dave,' she said. 'I don't want to quarrel with you. I came over here to say I'm sorry about what Barney did. I just wanted to bring Kitsy back, but he lost his temper.'

I didn't say a word. Anything I said would have been a mistake. So I just looked at her. She went on: 'We both love Kitsy, David. We want what's best for her, but I'm older and I ought to be a little wiser. In time you'll see I'm right and you'll be glad I did what I did the other night.'

She was a big, self-possessed woman, absolutely sure of herself, more sure than any human being had a right to be. I asked, 'Have you ever been wrong about anything, Bess?'

She whirled and walked away, shoulders stiff, her head high, and suddenly I realized Kitsy had been wrong telling Bess she'd sold her saddle. She was incapable of being a traitor to her people. Then the doubts came and I wasn't sure.

I stood alone, watching the shooting from the sidelines. My mother was in the schoolhouse helping the other women with the dinner. Both my father and Gil were shooting. Gil was decked out like a Christmas tree. He was wearing his green silk shirt with the white buttons, a brown-and-white calfskin vest decorated with silver *conchas*, his pearl-handled revolver, and spurs with big Mexican rowels. Everybody in the park had him pegged for a show-off, but he'd already established the fact that he could shoot. He'd won the tom turkey three years running.

The shoot lasted until noon, half of the contestants dropping out in the first round, with Gil, Bess, and Frank Dance the finalists. Gil won the tom, Bess the hen, and Frank said philosophically, 'Guess I got what the little boy shot at.'

Gil and Bess came in for some joshing about what would happen if they got hitched and ever started shooting at each other. 'Be a draw,' Matt Colohan said. 'They'd shoot each other between the eyes with the first volley.'

Gil winked at Bess, feeling proud of himself. 'Let's get hitched, Bess. We'll show 'em.'

Bess said, 'I'd better get inside where I belong and help get dinner.'

As she walked away, everybody gave Gil the laugh. Johnny Strong said, 'You need more'n dude duds to impress that girl.'

'Or fancy shooting,' Luke Jordan added.

'I'll show you some fancy shooting,' Gil said furiously. 'Elder, you got any potatoes?'

'I'll get them,' Elder Smith said, and went into his store.

We'd always had some off-the-cuff shooting after the turkey business had been settled, usually for a few good-natured side bets that didn't go over fifty cents. But Gil had never been able to take any rawhiding, and he couldn't now.

'Five dollars I can hit any potato that goes in the air,' Gil said.

'Hold on,' my father said. 'That's pretty steep.'

'Five dollars,' Gil said stubbornly.

Nobody took him up. When Elder Smith got back with the potatoes, the silence was so tight it squeaked. He looked around, not knowing what had happened. 'Here's your potatoes, Gil. I fetched a couple of tin cans if you want to—'

'Hell, nobody will bet with me,' Gil said. 'Boys, there's a gun in Buhl I want. A right fancy one with gold inlay on the barrels. You know, worked into a pattern of flowers and stuff like that. It'd go real good with my outfit, but I haven't got the price.' He pulled a gold eagle out of his pocket, held it up for everybody to see, then handed it to Elder Smith. 'Hold the stakes. Might as well make this worthwhile.' He dug a walnut out of another pocket and gave it to Frank Dance. 'Who'll cover my bet that I can hit it when Frank tosses it up? About fifteen feet high, Frank.'

Gil had a gift for currying folks the wrong way. It was enough to win the tom turkey, but to win it for the fourth time, and then rub in his superiority by trying to make money with his shooting was too much.

He looked around triumphantly. 'Anybody got enough grit to cover my bet?'

I didn't think Gil could do it and I doubted anyone else did. Kicking a tin can along the ground with every bullet in the gun, or hitting a potato thrown into the air was simple compared to smashing a walnut, as small as it was.

Finally Gil's arrogance won. Johnny Strong said, 'I'll cover your bet,' and handed Elder Smith ten dollars.

'I oughta have odds,' Gil said. No one offered any, so he brought another gold piece into view, holding it up between thumb and forefinger. 'If you won't give me odds, then make it worth shooting at.'

'I will,' Elder Smith said quietly.

'I'll be damned,' Gil said. 'A gambling preacher. All right, Elder, put up your money.'

Elder Smith held out his coin for Gil to see, and Gil gave his to him. Forty dollars riding on one shot! My brother had more gall than I had, even if I'd had twenty dollars to risk. In spite of myself, I felt a tingle of admiration for him.

Gil grinned, the picture of confidence. 'Throw it up, Frank.'

Dance threw the walnut into the air with an underarm toss. There was absolute silence as it curved up except for our breathing, then it reached the peak of the arc and seemed to pause. At that exact instant Gil fired, and the walnut disintegrated. Before the echoes of the shot died, Gil said, 'Pay up, Elder,' and held out his hand.

Elder Smith gave him the money, saying courteously, 'Congratulations, Gil.'

Nobody else congratulated him. I suppose both Johnny Strong and Elder Smith had wanted to teach him a lesson in humility, but it had backfired. As a family we might be down to our last ten cents, but Gil would buy that fancy gun in Buhl as sure as he was a foot high.

'Since you're the best shot in the park,' Frank Dance said, 'I guess you're our best fighting man.'

'Why, sure,' Gil said. 'You want any fighting

done, bring 'em on.'

'They're coming,' Dance said: 'The whole damned Rafter 3 crew.'

I think Dance saw the horsemen before he said anything about Gil being a fighting man, but I'm sure Gil hadn't. A dozen horsemen were coming up the road, Vic Toll in the lead. Then I was scared. The man riding beside him had his right arm in a sling. Sammy Blue, and I wasn't carrying my gun.

My father recognized Sammy Blue about the same time I did. He came to me, saying in a low voice, 'Hard to tell what this means, but don't start anything.'

'I can't even finish anything,' I said. 'I haven't got my gun.'

'A good thing,' he said.

Maybe it was. I didn't have any illusions about my ability with a gun, certainly not about the speed of my draw. Gil might have got the best of Blue, if he had the guts, but I wasn't sure he did. Anyhow, I couldn't ask him to take on my fight.

'I'll do the talking,' Elder Smith said, and moved toward the road so he could be the first man Toll would meet.

The Rafter 3 crew reined up a few feet in front of the Elder. Everyone but me had a gun because of the turkey shoot. It wouldn't take much to turn this into a battle, but I had the comforting thought that Toll didn't intend for it to be a fight or he wouldn't have ridden in this way.

'Good morning, neighbors,' Elder Smith said. 'Step down and join us. I think our Thanksgiving dinner is about ready.'

'Thank you kindly,' Toll said, 'but we ain't here to visit.' He looked us over, as coldly as a cattle buyer would size up a bunch of steers. 'I thought some of you might want to sell your spreads. Maybe all of you.'

'No,' Elder Smith said.

'That go for the rest of you?'

Everyone nodded, Matt Colohan bawling, 'You're damned right we ain't selling.'

Not one of the Rafter 3 riders looked like Gil. No fancy duds, I mean, or pearl-handled guns, but all of them had Winchesters in their boots and revolvers in the holsters on their hips. They were working cowhands, all except Sammy Blue, but they were tough, too, for that was the kind of men who gravitated to Vic Toll.

'I see,' Toll said softly. 'Well, don't forget we're offering to buy. That offer'll hold.' He paused, and added significantly, 'For a while.'

Without another word Toll swung his horse, Blue turning with him, and rode back down the line of riders, the others falling in behind him. Elder Smith wheeled and walked back to where I stood. His hands trembled but that was the only sign of nervousness he showed.

'Did you tell your father what Toll said to me that night before the meeting?' Elder Smith asked. I shook my head and he jerked his head at Pa. 'I want to talk to you, Joe.'

They moved away just as Bess came out of the schoolhouse banging on the bottom of a dishpan with a big spoon. She called, 'Come and get it before we throw it into the river.'

We walked toward her, Frank Dance saying: 'A dozen of 'em. Hell, they could clean this valley out in one night if they're a mind to.'

Matt Colohan, a little drunk on his own whiskey, said, 'Let's tackle 'em first.'

Dance shook his head. 'That'd be one way of committing suicide, Matt, and you know it.'

Johnny Strong said, 'I wonder who'll be the first to sell.'

No one tried to answer that question. We went inside. The seats had been moved to the walls, and the dinner was spread on tables formed by placing long planks on sawhorses. It looked good and smelled good, but I wasn't hungry and I doubted that anyone else was.

Now that it was over for the time being, Gil was cocky as ever. He said, loud enough for Bess to hear, 'If they'd started anything, I'd have got Toll.'

No one spoke. We waited until Elder Smith and my father came in. Elder Smith asked the blessing and we got into line behind the kids, our plates in our hands. We filled them and scattered outside to eat. I cleaned my plate up and went inside; then I noticed Bess was gone. I put my plate down, grabbed a slab of apple pie, and left the building, eating the pie out of my hand.

There was no way for me to know whether anyone else had seen Bess leave, and I didn't want to arouse suspicion by asking. I tightened the cinch, stepped into the saddle, and rode off, not answering Matt Colohan who yelled at me, 'Hey Dave, ain't you gonna wait for the dancing?'

I turned off the road at the Nordine lane, but I didn't go to the house. I turned around when I got about halfway up the lane. Vic Toll's big buckskin was tied in front of the Nordine house.

CHAPTER THIRTEEN

December was a cold month with an occasional light fall of snow. My father and I worked hard at the wood job, finishing a few days before Christmas. The cattle had been grazing on the lower slopes of Campbell Mountain, but now they began drifting toward the river, and Pa gave Gil the job of looking after them. Several times Gil had to haul hay, and twice he rode home with a new calf across the saddle, driving its mother in front of him.

Gil had changed. I wasn't sure why. Maybe he knew about Bess and Toll. Maybe she'd talked turkey to him. In any case, he spent far less time with her, and he worked at the job my father had given him, probably because he preferred riding to pulling a crosscut saw through a pine log.

Oh, he was still Gil, bragging at supper to my mother about something he had done, or how he was going away in the spring and get a job breaking horses for some rancher on the Yampa or maybe down on White River. She still gave him the biggest piece of pie at supper and she'd start the meat platter with him so he could take the choice piece, but it was a matter of degree. And he had quit calling me 'kid.'

My father changed, too, an insidious thing that I was slow to notice. Finally I realized he was afraid. He never talked about it. He didn't show it by being nervous and jumpy. But he took to wearing his gun when he worked, something he had never done. He didn't step out on the front porch just before he went to bed at night, as had been his habit. It was just that he was careful, even stopping the team part way up to where we were cutting wood. He'd sit motionless in the wagon studying the trees and stumps and boulders in front of him, and the dry washes that were like the deep lines on an old man's face. Then, apparently convinced there was no danger, he'd drive on.

We didn't talk much while we worked, but several nights, after supper, he seemed compelled to talk. Ma would sit with her legs stretched out to the fire while Gil was playing solitaire at the heavy-legged, graceless oak table in the center of the room. We bought most of Mrs. Jason's furniture when we moved to the park, and that table was included, no thing of beauty but serviceable.

My father was always figuring, usually at the other end of the table from Gil. Several times he'd say, 'I'm going into Buhl right after the first of the year and see how much money I can borrow. We've got to get these scrub bulls off our range.'

Horrified, Ma would say, 'Joe, you're not going to borrow money. You know what bankers are. Isn't it enough that some night we'll be murdered in our beds by those Rafter 3 cutthroats without having to worry about bankers?'

This, I knew, was the very thing my father was worrying about. His face would go very grave, his lips tightening under his bristly mustache, then he would say, 'You've got to use money to make money, Sadie.' He'd go to bed then. I guess he just couldn't stand her nagging.

A couple of nights before the Christmas program in the schoolhouse, he got down to brass tacks. This time he talked directly to me. I thought I understood. Gil might leave in the spring to break horses for someone else, or go to work for Bess, but I was the one who would stay. I hadn't ever mentioned leaving home again, and I believe he sensed that it had been a natural boyish spirit of rebellion that had burst out in me like a lighted piece of pitch pine and now had burned itself out.

'We've got limited range,' my father said, 'as long as the Rafter 3 holds the present line, and it's a cinch they won't give up any of their grass; that means all of us in the park will be held to the size herds we've got now, so good bulls is our only way of expanding. We'll get more weight on each steer.'

He figured some more, frowned, and chewed on the end of his pencil. He leaned back and looked at me. Gil kept on playing solitaire, and Ma went on sewing. As long as my father didn't mention borrowing money, she let him talk. At last he threw his pencil down on the table. 'But damn it, how can you talk sense to a hard head like Matt Colohan? No use of any of us putting good bulls on the range if all of us don't. Maybe I can borrow enough to loan Matt—'

'There you go, Joe,' my mother cut in. 'I was just waiting to hear that. Borrowing money to loan it to a whiskey-making old soak like Matt Colohan is the stupidest thing I ever heard you say.'

She looked at him as if daring him to argue with her, but he didn't. He got up and grinned at me as if to say he knew I understood, then he went to bed. A moment later I did, too, but I lay awake a long time, stirred up inside in a way I hadn't been since I'd talked to Elder Smith. My father had realized his big dream to own a ranch, but he was not a man who would ever quit dreaming. Now I had a queer feeling he was afraid something was going to happen to him and he wanted to pass his dream on to me.

The day before Christmas a saddle tramp drifted in. A little, middle-aged man with a wistful smile and a droopy mustache, he was pretty typical. Failure was written all over him. At this time of year he should have been five hundred miles south of here.

My father didn't like to put strangers up, but he couldn't very well say No. Anyhow, this was Christmas. The fellow said his name was Jones, he'd been working in Montana and he was trying to get to Arizona where he had a job waiting for him on a ranch just out of Tucson. It was an old yarn that none of us believed, but Pa told him to put his horse in the corral and come in for supper. He did, and the amount of food he put down was unbelievable.

After supper we started getting ready to go to the program at the schoolhouse and Pa decided Jones had to go with us. Jones didn't want to go. He'd just be in our way, he said, and he didn't know anybody. 'Go ahead and have a good time,' he finished. 'I'll make my bed in the haymow and I'll get started at sunup. I'm beholden to you folks enough now.'

'Let him stay here,' I said. 'He's right. He won't enjoy the program.'

My father's face tightened. For a minute I thought he was going to blow up. Then he said in a low tone, a tone nobody but Ma ever argued with, 'By God, Jones, you're going or you're dragging out of here.'

I was a little irritated with my father. This fellow Jones was about as harmless looking a man as you could imagine. All he wanted was a meal which he would make do for a couple of days, or until he found another ranch where he could eat again. In the morning he'd be on his way, and we'd never see him again. But there wasn't anything I could do, with Pa's mind made up, so Jones went with us.

We never had enough seats in the schoolhouse on Christmas Eve. Ma got one, but the rest of us stood up with the other men along the sides and rear of the room. I always got a tingle out of Christmas. We never made much of it ourselves, mostly because we'd drifted when Gil and I were kids. We didn't have the money, anyhow. But here in the park the Christmas program was one of the big events of the year, and almost everybody came. I'd always looked forward to it when Kitsy was here, and I was a little surprised to realize I was anticipating it again.

Maybe it was the age-old Christmas carols that did something to me, or the program itself with the recitations and the Christmas story from the Bible and the manger scene that the older children performed for us. I remembered Kitsy and I had been in it the year I was in school. Elder Smith was as patient with his pupils as any woman, and he performed miracles with them. Bess always helped with the Christmas program, and I had to grudgingly admit there just wasn't anything that woman couldn't do.

But this year I couldn't get into the spirit. I thought about this fellow Jones. The more I thought, the less I liked it. His story was purely phony. A saddle bum headed for Tucson would never wander into Dillon's Park. He'd go right on south from Buhl to White River and on to the Grand from there. Or he'd be over in Utah fifty or a hundred miles to the west of us. But he sure as hell wouldn't be here, with the canyon of the Big Red blocking him to the south.

By the time the program was over and we got home, I was in a dither, but I didn't want my father to know. I wasn't at all sure what Jones would or could do, but I didn't think he was a killer. Of course, he could fire the barn if he slept in the mow, and I remembered what Elder Smith had said about Toll using bullets and a torch.

I put the team away, and when I got in the house, my mother asked where the guinea hen was she'd told me to catch earlier in the day. I'd forgotten all about it. She was put out at me and said I'd better go get the hen now.

'I don't know where they're roosting,' I said. 'I'll get her in the morning if I have to shoot her.'

101

My mother sniffed her disapproval. 'And tear her all to pieces so there won't be any breast.'

'I'll shoot her head off,' I promised. 'Or get Gil to.'

'*One* of you boys had better, or we won't have a Christmas dinner,' she grumbled.

'Ma, make Jones a bed here on the couch,' I said. 'It's cold in the haymow and this is Christmas.'

'That ain't necessary,' Jones said. 'I'll sleep in the mow if I have my druthers.'

He was bent over the heater, his hands held out. The ride home from the schoolhouse had chilled him to the bone. He was about as pathetic looking a saddle bum as I'd ever seen, and we'd had some dandies.

Ma started to object, but my father said quickly, 'You fix him up in here, Sadie. He'll freeze to death outside. You're staying for breakfast, too, Jones.'

Jones didn't seem as appreciative as he should have been, but he didn't object very strenuously, so my mother got some quilts out of her bedroom and made his bed.

Gil had stayed at the schoolhouse to ride home with Bess, so he didn't come in for another hour or so. I was asleep, but I stirred enough to hear him shut the back door. Later, with the night still pit-black, I heard the guinea hens. I turned over, mentally cursing them and knowing Kitsy wouldn't be out there tonight.

102

As far as I was concerned, I'd put every guinea hen we had in the pot tomorrow if Ma would let me, but she always said they were the best protection against hawks we could get because they always sounded the alarm to the chickens.

I stayed awake a few minutes, thinking of the time I'd heard the guinea hens and right after that Kitsy had tapped on my window. Then I got to wondering if it was going to snow some more. We'd had about an inch a couple of days ago and it hadn't all gone off. We were in for a hard winter, some of the old-timers said, but so far it hadn't come.

The next thing I knew someone fired a gun in front of the house. It was still dark, for the sun came up late on the twenty-fifth of December and the clouds had been low and forbidding when we'd come in the night before, so I didn't have any idea what time it was.

I pulled on my boots, not even putting on my socks, and ran through the house in my underclothes. Ma stood in the bedroom doorway, a lighted lamp in her hand. 'Pa just went out to milk—'

I didn't wait to hear what she had to say. I yanked the door open and ran out into the bitter cold. Pa was flat on his belly. From the grotesque way he lay there, I didn't have to turn him over to know he was dead. I heard Ma scream. I plunged back into the house and whirled to look at the couch.

Jones was gone.

CHAPTER FOURTEEN

I ran through the house and into Gil's bedroom. I threw the covers back and shook him awake. 'Get up,' I said. 'Pa's been shot. Get up.' He blinked at me as if unable to grasp what I'd said. 'Get up,' I repeated, and when he still lay there, I took hold of his ankles and dragged his legs off the bed and dropped them so his feet hit the cold floor instead of the rag rug.

As I ran through the kitchen into my room, I heard my mother crying hysterically in the front part of the house. I dressed as fast as I could, buckled on my gun belt, wrapped my muffler around my neck, and pulled on my sheepskin. The only rifle we had was my father's Winchester hanging across two pegs just inside the kitchen door. I grabbed it as I ran out of the house and went on across the yard to the barn. I had no thought beyond catching the man who had murdered my father, and time was the only thing right then that mattered.

Before I finished saddling my horse, a scarlet sunrise was flaming across the horizon to the east above the sagebrush plateau. When I reined up in front of the house, the light was strong enough for me to see where the killer had stood not more than twenty feet from the door. Half a dozen brown paper cigarette stubs were on the ground. He must have waited quite a while.

I rode in widening circles, feeling the pressure of time, but wanting to know where Jones had left his horse. He would have saddled the animal and tied him not far from where he'd waited. The ground where I found the cigarette stubs was bare and frozen hard, so there were no boot tracks, but I found horse tracks in a patch of snow at the end of our lane. I stepped down and took a moment to study them. The sign indicated the animal had been tied there for some time, a couple of hours, at least. At the edge of the snow I found the sharp clear print of a big boot. The heel was not run over on the side. The killer was wearing a fairly new pair.

I swung back into the saddle and put my horse down the lane in a run. When I reached the road, I stopped, suddenly realizing I was being foolish because I might have to ride all day. Wearing my horse out the first hour in the morning was no good. I wished I hadn't taken time to look at the tracks.

Jones was my man. All I had to do was find him. Pulling out in the middle of the night and not staying for breakfast as my father had asked him to. His phony story about heading for Tucson but he just happened to wander into the park. Why hell, there wasn't any doubt about it. Toll had hired a killer and Jones was the man.

Now the question was which way he had turned. He would stay on the road to put as much distance as he could between him and the man he'd killed, and in the shortest possible time. He couldn't ride fast across the fenced hay meadows or along the river, where it was brushy and there were patches of ice. But I had no way of guessing whether he'd head upriver and try to get out of the park and escape into Wyoming or Utah, or whether he'd try for the Rafter 3 and hope Vic Toll would hide him out.

I wasted time, half an hour maybe, before I picked up fresh sign to the north that told me he was making a run for it upriver. So I headed that way, knowing that by now he must have almost an hour's start on me. But I felt better when I remembered Jones's horse was a small, mouse-colored gelding that looked as if it were on its last legs. A horse's appearance can be deceiving, but I didn't think I'd been fooled by this animal. I'd catch the bastard before he got out of the park.

More than that, I knew the country. The road petered out at Johnny Strong's ranch. That was the end of the park, too. North of there the Big Red boiled down through a ten-mile canyon, and Jones would have to leave the river and fight his way around the canyon through wild country broken by a dozen dry washes feeding into the Big Red. His horse would be finished by noon.

So I took a steady, ground-eating pace, confident I'd have my man within a few hours. The sun was up, but the clouds still hung low above the plateau so the light was as thin as it would be at dusk. Elder Smith was cutting wood behind the store as I rode past. I pulled in long enough to say, 'Pa was murdered this morning.'

Elder Smith was too shocked to do anything but stand there and look at me. I asked, 'Will you let the Dances know? And Bess?'

'I'll tell them,' he said in a voice choked with emotion. 'I didn't think it would be Joe. I was sure I'd be the one.'

I rode on, glad that the neighbors would be told. Elder Smith would help out. My mother and Gil would need him. Death was something I knew nothing about. This was the first time it had ever hit close to me. I wasn't sure what all had to be done, but the body would have to be laid out. The eyes closed. Pennies placed over them, I'd heard. Someone would dress Pa in his Sunday clothes. I suppose people would say I should have stayed, but this was the thing I had to do.

I kept on, straight up the river. The sun, which seemed to add no warmth to the chill day, climbed higher into the sky. The clouds had broken away, and now my steadily shortening shadow rode beside me. I passed Matt Colohan's ranch. No sign of life. He was the worst rancher in the park, with a fat, slovenly wife and eight kids. He never worked any more than he had to, making most of his living from his still. His calf crop was always poor, and he never had more than ten or fifteen steers to market in the fall, but he never worried. He was half-drunk most of the time, and he certainly would have been last night, it being Christmas Eve.

I passed the March ranch. Luke Jordan's. Sam Binford. Riley MacKay. All of them set back off the road to my right at the base of Campbell Mountain. I tried not to think about my father, or about what would happen to us now. To Gil, who had always been babied; to my mother who wouldn't know what to do; to me, who had found something here in the park I had never known before, something that was of value as I'd worked beside my father, knowing the Big Ten was ours, and that some day it would be mine. Not Gil's because he didn't want it.

Suddenly tears began running down my cheeks. I didn't ask for them. They were just there, and the lump that was in my throat was so big I couldn't swallow. I was ashamed and I was glad no one was here to see me cry. I couldn't remember when I'd shed any tears. Maybe I never had. Ma used to talk about it. Gil cried so much, but I didn't, she said. Gil used to hurt me when we fought. He'd hurt me like hell, but I'd never cried.

No, I mustn't think about my father. I'd

think about that murdering bastard who had eaten our food and slept on our couch and fed his horse our hay, and then, had stood outside in the cold and shot my father when he'd come out of the house with a milk bucket in his hand.

And I'd think what I'd do to that son of a bitch when I caught him. I'd kill him. I'd twist his God-damned neck until he was purple in the face and he couldn't talk. Murder? Hell, no. We made our own law out here. We stomped our own snakes. We didn't depend on fat old Ed Veach to bring the law of Marion County to Dillon's Park.

Now I was past Johnny Strong's ranch, and there was no road, just a stock trail that wound up the cliff ahead of me like the wiggling track of a snake. I could hear the roar of the Big Red pounding down through the canyon above me.

Pulling up, I tipped my head back and studied the cliff. In places I could see the trail. In other places I couldn't, but here it was higher and colder than it was at the lower end of the park, and snow lay in a solid carpet on the ground six inches or more deep. No tracks! Jones hadn't come this way. I'd just been riding along, certain that he was ahead of me, thinking about every God-damned thing except what I should have been.

Slowly I turned my horse and rode back, wondering if Jones could have left the road somewhere and angled across a shoulder of Campbell Mountain to the trail that led up the cliff and around the canyon of the Big Red. No, I didn't think so. Not knowing the country, he'd stick to the road as long as he could. Besides, this end of Campbell Mountain was covered by brush, a steep, broken country that would raise hell with Jones's old horse. No, I was sure he hadn't done anything as foolish as that, but what had he done?

I turned in at Johnny Strong's place just on the chance he'd seen Jones ride by. I didn't realize how cold I was until I was inside the house and standing beside the red-hot heater. I told Johnny what had happened, holding my hands out to the stove, rubbing them and working my toes in my boots. They didn't have much feeling. Maybe they were frozen.

Johnny was young, not over thirty, a slender, rawhide-tough man who had ridden for Rafter 3. He'd quit just after Toll was made foreman. He didn't make any bones about it. He couldn't stand the bastard, he'd said, and he still couldn't. He had been, along with Elder Smith, my father's best friend. Now he stood staring blankly at me like a man who had been knocked cold but is still on his feet.

Mrs. Strong, who had been nursing a baby in the kitchen, heard what I said, and she ran into the room, the baby in her arms. 'Johnny, hitch up the buggy. I'll go right down.'

'No,' I said. 'There's no need of that. Bess and Lorna Dance will be there. We'll let you know when the funeral is.'

'He's right,' Johnny said. 'You've got a little cold, anyhow. You don't want to dry up with that baby doing as well as he is.' He turned to where his coat and hat hung on the wall. 'I'll go with you, Dave—just to keep you from murdering that devil in case you find him.'

'Murder him?' I stared at Johnny, not understanding. 'It wouldn't be murder. It'd be an execution.'

'I know it and you know it, but Ed Veach won't. He'll see you hang just to please Vic Toll if nothing else.' He slipped into his coat and crossed back to where I stood. 'If a man wants to get his neck stretched, it's usually his own business.' He put a hand on my shoulder. 'In your case it ain't. We need you, and we're gonna need you a hell of a lot more before this is over. You've got a lot of Joe in you, Dave.'

I turned away from him and headed for the door. The damned tears started running down my face again.

I waited outside until Johnny saddled up and joined me. As we rode downriver, Johnny said: 'Dave, this is like looking for a needle in a haystack. He might have circled on you after he headed this way, just to throw you off the track.'

'He might have, all right,' I said.

I hadn't thought of that, but it could have been easy enough, with the ground frozen and the snow scattered in patches the way it was at the other end of the park. I felt like a fool. By this time that devil might be halfway to Buhl or warming his hands in the Rafter 3 bunkhouse.

'We'll watch the side of the road for tracks,' Johnny said. 'He might have turned off anywhere.'

Not up here, I thought, but I didn't argue. We rode slowly, each watching his side of the road. Presently Johnny said, 'Ed Veach has got to know about this.' I grunted an agreement, not caring whether Ed Veach knew or not. Then Johnny said, 'Let's stop at the March place and send Hugo to town.'

'I'll go on,' I said. 'You tell him.'

He turned off and joined me a few minutes later. 'Hugo will go soon as he eats,' he said.

The snow had gradually thinned as we dropped downriver. By the time we reached Matt Colohan's ranch it was so spotty that a man could have turned back anywhere without leaving tracks. It was all a lot of damn foolishness anyway, because if he had turned back he'd have done it sooner than this.

I should have got Frank Dance up. He was the best tracker in the park. He wouldn't have ridden to hell an' gone on a wild goose chase the way I'd done. He could pick up a fly's track on a pane of glass, or so folks said. I would have gone after Dance if I hadn't been so sure I knew what Jones would do.

I was mentally kicking myself all over the place when Johnny said, 'Dave, what color horse was that yahoo forking?'

'A mouse.'

'Looks to me like that's it yonder in Matt's corral. Least-wise I never seen it before.'

I looked up. 'That's it,' I said, and dug in my spurs. I headed across Matt Colohan's hay meadow. He had more fence down than he had up, so I rode straight to the house, Johnny a jump behind. I hit the ground running and plunged across the porch and jerked the door open, not taking time to knock.

Matt was sitting on one of his homemade chairs, a jug in his hand. His fat wife had her mouth open, jawing him about something. Kids were all over the place, some of them bigger than Jones. Matt and his wife both straightened up and looked at me, bug-eyed. Then I saw Jones back in the corner and I went for him, the kids scattering in front of me and heading for the kitchen like cowhands coming home to dinner.

Jones let out a blast like a scared sheep; then I got hold of him and yanked him out of his chair and hit him. He went back about ten feet and fell. I jumped on top of him and got my thumbs on his throat and started to squeeze. He squirmed around and hit at me; he started kicking the floor and trying to get loose, but by the time Matt and Johnny pulled me off, his face was getting purple.

'Dave, what'd I tell you?' Johnny bellowed. 'They can hang him in Buhl just as well as you can choke him to death out here.'

'What the hell's going on?' Matt demanded, shocked sober.

Jones was sitting up, rubbing his throat and trying to get his breath. Matt had me by one arm and Johnny by the other, and after a while I quit struggling. I'd lost my head. Johnny was right, of course.

'I want to know what's going on,' Matt said again.

'That bastard shot and killed Pa this morning,' I said, so choked up my words were almost incoherent. 'Let me go. I'm all right now.'

Matt began to swear. Then he stopped. 'This morning, you say, Dave?'

'Yeah, this morning. About six, I guess it was.'

'Then you've got the wrong man, boy. This galoot showed up here about four, and he's been here ever since.'

CHAPTER FIFTEEN

I walked to the corner of the room and sat down in the chair Jones had been in. I said, 'Matt, you're drunk.'

'I ain't no such thing,' Colohan said hotly. 'Oh, I've had a nip or two, but I don't never get drunk. This here hombre pounded on the front door while it was darker'n the inside of a bull's

114

gut. I lit a lamp and looked at the clock yonder. Five minutes after four.'

'That's right,' Mrs. Colohan said. 'He woke the baby up. I had to get out of bed and fix him a sugar tit to suck on so he'd quit hollering and go back to sleep.'

Jones got up off the floor and found another chair. He took a pipe out of his pocket and began to fill it. He said sullenly, 'I dunno why you've got to bust in here and start choking me to death. I didn't do nothing to your pa. I waited till your folks was asleep, then I got up and left.'

I watched Jones fill and light his pipe. I felt like hell. The Colohans wouldn't lie about a thing like this. Matt might have been drunk, but his wife wouldn't have been. Then I remembered the cigarette stubs I had found where the killer had waited outside.

I crossed the room to where Jones sat and held out the makings to him. 'Have a cigarette,' I said. 'I guess you ran out of papers or you wouldn't be nursing a pipe.'

Affronted, he said, 'Why the hell shouldn't I nurse a pipe? I don't like cigarettes. Damned paper gets wet and the tobacco gets into my mouth. I don't smoke nothing but a pipe.'

I looked at his boots. Both heels were sadly run over on the sides. Jones wasn't my father's killer, and all I'd done was to waste the day chasing after the wrong man. I asked, 'What'd he say when he opened the door, Matt?'

115

'Something about could he sleep in the barn. He'd already put his horse in the corral. I remembered seeing him at the schoolhouse with you folks, so I said I thought he was staying at the Munros and he says no, he just had supper there. Claimed he couldn't go on because he was cold. Frozed his feet—'

I was getting madder by the minute. I broke into Colohan's talk. 'Matt, he's a liar. When I went to bed, he was on the couch, snug as hell.' I got up and put my hand on the butt of my gun. 'Jones, you're into this up to your neck. You'd better tell us...'

'Hold on, boy, hold on,' Jones begged. 'I'll tell you all I can, but it ain't much.'

I sat down again. I had aimed to scare him and I had, but I was convinced that if he'd had any part in my father's murder it had not been by intent. He'd probably been sucked in by someone who had planned this killing for a long time.

'Let's hear your spiel,' I said.

'Like I told your folks, I was headed for Arizona where I've got a job waiting,' Jones said, 'but I had some bad luck in Rock Springs and lost all my money in a poker game. Lost my gun, too. I noticed a little gent watching me all the time I was playing. When I walked out of the saloon, this gent trails along—'

'What'd he look like?' I asked.

He blinked at me. 'Oh, I dunno. Had mean eyes. I noticed that. Looked like a gunslinger.

116

I've seen his kind. Kill a man just as soon as look—'

'Did he carry his right arm in a sling?' I asked.

Jones scratched an ear as he thought about it. 'No, but that right arm was stiff. I seen that, all right. Everything he done he done with his left hand.'

I looked at Johnny Strong. 'Sammy Blue,' I said, and Johnny nodded. 'Go on,' I said to Jones.

'Well, this gent followed me out of the saloon. He comes up and says, "How'd you like to earn fifty dollars?" Fifty dollars looked like a million, so I said sure. He tells me 'bout this Dillon's Park and how I was to get here. I was to show up at the first house, belonged to a feller named Munro he said, and ask to stay overnight. I'd get twenty-five dollars then and the other twenty-five would be mailed to me in Buhl.'

'That all?' I asked.

He started pulling on his pipe, discovered it had gone cold, and fished a match out of his vest pocket. 'Yeah, except for one little thing that was kind o' funny. He says to leave Munro's place after they're asleep. He says that's what I was getting paid for, to not be there by three, four in the morning. I asked why, and he said just do what I was told.'

'Hell's bells,' Matt Colohan yelled. 'That Blue hombre was setting him up for a hanging.'

117

Jones's mouth fell open, his slow mind finally catching on to what had happened to him. 'That dirty booger!' He swallowed. 'If I hadn't stopped here, you'd have figgered I done it.'

I got up, sick with disappointment and frustration. Sammy Blue knew he might be traced if we caught Jones, so he'd probably stayed out of the state. We'd never get him into Colorado. If he was questioned, he'd deny he ever saw Jones, and that would be good enough for Ed Veach.

'Tell Hugo to take Jones to town,' I told Johnny. 'Maybe Veach will hold him and get something else out of him.'

'I don't figger he will,' Johnny said, 'but I'll have Hugo take him in.'

I left the house, mounted, and went home. The short December day was over and I rode through darkness. When I reached our lane, I saw there was a light in the house and I wondered if Ma and Gil were home; but when I went in I saw that Frank Dance was there, and that my father had been laid out in a coffin that rested on two sawhorses in the front room.

'Howdy, Dave,' Dance said.

I nodded at him and stood beside the coffin for a time, looking at my father's face. He was dressed in his boiled shirt and tie and store suit, as I knew he would be. His hair was combed and someone had shaved him. He looked serene and peaceful, but it wasn't him. It just wasn't him. I turned away and walked into the kitchen.

Dance followed me. He said: 'There's coffee on the stove. Lorna fetched an apple pie over, and Bess, she made some sandwiches. They're wrapped in that cloth on the table.'

I didn't think I was hungry, but Dance understood how it was. He went ahead and poured a cup of coffee and cut a piece of pie, and by the time he opened up the sandwiches I remembered I hadn't eaten all day. I was famished.

'Elder Smith was here most all day,' Dance said. 'We'll have the funeral tomorrow afternoon. We'll get the grave dug in the morning.' He was silent for a time, then he added: 'Elder Smith is a real help in time of trouble. He's lived here a long time, longer'n any of the rest of us except the Nordines. He's preached to us and baptized our children and taught 'em in school and even done some doctorin'. Them damned doctors in Rock Springs charge $150 to come out here, you know. Hell, we can't afford that, so we've made do, with the Elder helping out.'

'Where's Ma and Gil?'

'Over at Nordine's. Shortly, he's coming over after 'while and he'll sit up the rest of the night.' He cleared his throat. 'Your ma took it right hard, Dave, but I reckon she'll get over it in time.' He looked down at the floor, and then he broke out: 'My God, what are we going to do, Dave? A man gets shot coming out of his front door on Christmas morning! Where'll they stop? Who'll be next?'

He began to cry. He turned his back, ashamed to show his feelings, I suppose. I sat there at the table, my hands fisted. Frank Dance was the strongest man in the park, short and squat, with tremendous shoulders and hands twice as big as mine. I had seen him get under a loaded wagon that had broken a wheel and boost it up by himself so another wheel could be slipped into place. If there was a man in the park who had a right to be called a man, it was Frank Dance, and yet he was crying for my father.

Pa had lived here three years, just three years after all that time he'd drifted around. This was the first home he'd known since he was married at nineteen, my age, but those three years had been long enough to earn the respect and affection of every man in the park. Three years of owning a piece of land and living the way he wanted to live and dreaming the dreams that he had nourished for so long and never really thought he could make come true. Now it was gone. And for what?

I got up and began walking around the kitchen, my hands opening and clenching at my sides. Dance wiped a sleeve across his eyes and turned around. 'I thought maybe you'd tell me but you haven't, so I've got to ask. Did you get that bastard?'

120

'He wasn't the one,' I said, and told him what I'd done. 'I should have gone after you in the first place, but no, I had to do it myself.'

'Don't blame yourself, Dave,' he said quickly. 'I'd have done the same if it had been me. They must have been figuring on this for a long time. They knew what Joe done, leaving by the front door like that. Usually a man goes out through the kitchen door.'

'Pa did that because he didn't want to wake me and Gil till he had to,' I said. 'Especially Gil. Ma always claimed he was a light sleeper, so Pa said it wasn't any trouble to go out through the front.'

'How did that killing son of a bitch know that?'

'Yeah,' I said. 'How did he?'

'Why don't you go to bed, Dave? This has been a bad day, and tomorrow won't be no easier.'

I went to bed, but I couldn't sleep. I knew the answer to Dance's question. Whoever had killed my father was a park man. He had to be to know a little detail like coming out the front door. From now on, every time I looked at a neighbor, I'd wonder if he was the murderer.

CHAPTER SIXTEEN

Everyone who lived in the park attended my father's funeral except Barney Lux and Johnny Strong's wife who was in bed with her cold, and Hugo March who had not got back from Buhl. Tears were shed that day. A lot of them. Even by Bess. Elder Smith choked up twice during the service. But the worst of all was the final minute after we heard the last hymn and the last prayer, and Frank Dance and Matt Colohan picked up shovels and began filling the grave, some of the clods frozen so hard they sounded like rocks hitting the coffin.

Gil and Bess were standing together on the other side of the grave, my mother beside me. Suddenly I realized that I had my arm around her and she was crying, her head against my side. I couldn't stand the banging of those frozen clods against the coffin, and I led my mother away, down the slope to the rigs below the cemetery.

Bess had brought us in her hack. Shorty Quinn was already in the front seat holding the lines. I gave my mother a hand, and she stepped into the back seat. Bess sat beside her and Gil got in front with Shorty. I started to get in, when I heard Johnny Strong call, 'Dave.'

I turned and waited as he came down the slope in long strides. He motioned for me to come to him, so I stepped away from the hack. When he reached me, he said in a low tone, 'We'll be having a meeting before long.' I nodded, and then he said, 'Got ary notion yet who done it?'

If I could trust any man in the park, it would be Johnny Strong. Maybe I should tell him that my father's murderer was right in the park, someone we all knew, probably a man who had attended the funeral, a pallbearer, maybe one of the men who was filling the grave this very moment.

No, I wouldn't tell him, I decided. I trusted him, but he might tell someone he trusted, and in time everyone in the park would know what I thought. I'd wait, and someday I'd find out, and when I did I'd take care of the bastard myself.

'No,' I told Johnny. 'No notion at all.'

'Watch yourself, Dave,' he said. 'This ain't over.'

When we got home, I stepped out and helped my mother down. Bess asked, 'Is there anything I can do, Mrs. Munro?'

'Nothing more than you have done,' my mother said. 'You've been awfully kind.'

She went into the house. Gil said, 'I'll come over after while,' and Bess said, 'You do that.'

After Gil had followed my mother into the house, Bess said, 'Dave, I want to be your friend. You're mad at me because of Kitsy, and the way Barney treated you that night, but we're neighbors and we've got to work together. You'll be taking Joe's place, not Gil.'

I looked at Bess, this big woman who was good in a lot of ways and who had her soft side. I had seen it today. But she was stubborn and I didn't think she would ever change. I said, 'We'll get along. As far as Kitsy's concerned, it's just the same as it was. I'll marry her.'

I walked into the house, and I didn't look back, but I heard the pound of shod hoofs and the rattle of wheels on the hard ground. No, Bess would never change, I thought, but neither would I and neither would Kitsy.

Gil was building a fire in the kitchen range, and I built one in the heater. Then I changed my clothes. Ma huddled in a chair in the front room, her hands folded on her lap, staring ahead into space and seeing nothing. Gil went out through the back door and chopped wood for a while. I wandered through the house, seeing things that had belonged to my father that reminded me of him: The Winchester I had carried yesterday, his Colt and gun belt, boots and spurs, his weather-stained Stetson and leather coat that hung on the wall just inside the back door.

I had a strange feeling the house was deserted, but I think that what I really missed was the absence of any one who could command. It would be worse in the morning. Who would give the orders for the day? Who would decide whether we fixed the fence that was down between us and Anchor? Or would we cut the pigs that were almost too big to hold already? Would we haul gravel from the river for the corrals, now that the ground was frozen and we could get to the gravel bed?

I picked up the milk bucket in the pantry and went out to milk. It was dusk, a little early, but I was restless and it gave me something to do. Milking would be my job. Gil would dry our Jersey up in a week if he milked. I knew that was the truth and not just an excuse. Right there was the problem. Gil had worked pretty well the last few weeks, but I had no faith that it would last.

When I went back into the house, Ma had supper ready. She had set a plate for Pa and pulled his chair up to the table! I was startled. When I looked at Gil, I saw he was, too. It wouldn't have surprised me if Ma had put food on his plate, but she didn't. So we ate, with the haunting feeling that my father's ghost was there at the table with us.

When we finished picking at our food, and that was about all we did, I asked, 'What are we going to do?'

'I don't know,' my mother said. 'I've been asking myself that, but I—I just can't think.'

Gil took the makings from his vest pocket and began to roll a cigarette. He was looking at the brown paper, not at me or Ma when he said, 'I'm leaving in the morning.'

Ma's face turned white. I guess mine did,

too. I was that surprised. Ma said, 'You can't, Gil. It's wintertime. You'd get sick. I wouldn't be there ...' She stopped and bowed her head, her hands tightly clasped on her lap. I thought for the first time she realized she was talking to a son who was nearly twenty-three.

'I guess that's why I've got to go, Ma.' Gil looked up as he put the cigarette into his mouth. His dark brown hair was pointing in every direction as if he had been running a hand through it all evening; his handsome face showed his worry. 'Bess has been telling me I've got to get out of the park, and she's the one that counts with me.'

'It takes two to run this outfit,' I said.

'You can hire Kip Dance,' he said. 'He's a good worker.'

'You wouldn't leave just because Bess told you to,' Ma said. 'There must be some other reason.'

'Yeah, there is.' Gil looked at me. 'And you know what it is.'

I wasn't sure. I said, 'Somebody's got to do the figuring and planning and give the orders, and you don't want me to do it. That it?'

'I won't take your orders, but that wasn't what I meant. I just ain't no good at these ranch hand things and you are. If I dig a posthole, the damned thing goes slonchwise. If I'm building fence, the wire busts. If I drive a staple into a post, it comes out the first time a cow leans on it.' He shook his head at me. 'It

126

wouldn't work, Dave.'

He was right. He was the most inept man in the park when it came to doing the kind of thing he was talking about. I had a little glimmer of understanding then. Maybe it wasn't just that he was lazy or had taken advantage of Ma's excuses for him to get out of work. He was overburdened with pride, and maybe it was the fear of losing face, of failing to do the simple things well that had made him act the way he had.

I didn't say anything, and neither did Ma. Gil went on, 'I'll get a job breaking horses on some big outfit on the Yampa or White River or out in Utah. If I don't catch on, I'll take a shot at catching and breaking wild horses. A man can make good money that way if he's lucky.' He got up and put on his coat. 'I'm going over to tell Bess good-bye.'

After he left, my mother began clearing the table. I went into the front room, got a tablet, a pen, and bottle of ink off the big oak table and returned to the kitchen. My mother was pouring hot water from the teakettle into the dishpan when I sat down. She filled the kettle at the pump and set it back on the stove. Then she came to the table.

She said, 'Dave.'

I looked up at her. Her lips were tightly pressed, and she was blinking, trying to hold back the tears. 'Dave, I guess you thought I was foolish to set your father's plate that way and put his chair up to the table, but I thought maybe he knew. Maybe he could see. We didn't have any flowers to take to the funeral. I wanted to do something to show my respect. I guess I wanted to tell him I was sorry.'

My mother had always turned to Gil, never to me, but now it was different. Gil was leaving, and I was all she had. I didn't know what to say, because this business of my father looking down from wherever he was and seeing his plate and chair was not a thing I could believe.

'Joe married beneath him and had to leave home,' she said in a low voice. 'He was nineteen and I was seventeen, and I was scared because we didn't have anything.'

She whirled and went back to the stove. 'You're going to stay, Dave?'

'Sure, I'll stay.'

'You're the steady one, Dave. You always have been. You've been the strong one, too. I never had to worry about you. Whatever happens you can take care of yourself, but Gil can't. Joe said it was the way I raised you boys. Maybe it was, and if it was, then God forgive me for what I've done to Gil.'

That was all she said. She washed and dried the dishes, her hair brushed straight back from her forehead and pinned in a tight little bun at the back of her head. She was still wearing the black satin dress she had worn to the funeral, the only good dress she owned. This was the first time I had ever seen her work in the kitchen in that dress. Always before, she had taken it off the moment she got home from church.

When she was done, she went to bed, and a cold and lonely bed it would be. Maybe she hadn't been a wife to my father. Maybe that was what she wanted to tell him she was sorry about. Still, they had been used to each other. They'd have had to be, married for almost twenty-four years. Now it was behind her. She was alone. Tomorrow Gil would be gone. Just me, then, and maybe I'd be shot going out through the front door sometime just as my father had been.

I wrote a long letter to Kitsy that night, trying to tell her how much I loved her, how much I wanted to marry her. Something had happened to me today. I couldn't put it into words, but I hoped she could feel it. I had been a boy the night she'd got me out of bed to run away, but I was a man now. I was ready for marriage. I wanted her, wanted her as I had never dreamed I could, and even after I went to bed I lay awake, filled with that same want.

CHAPTER SEVENTEEN

Gil left the next morning, he didn't wear his fancy duds, his expensive Justins, his green silk

129

shirt, the calfskin vest with the silver *cochas*: he left all that foofaraw in his room. When he reined his sorrel up outside the kitchen door and stepped down, he looked like any bronc twister hunting a job. He was even wearing Pa's gun instead of his.

Ma came out of the kitchen carrying a small canvas bag that jingled as she walked. Gil seldom had any money, although he hadn't been to town since Thanksgiving, so maybe he still had the $40 he'd won at the turkey shoot. I'd already talked to Ma about money because I knew my father had had about $200 left from the sale of our steers in the fall. That was all we would have until fall, and I'd told Ma before breakfast that she simply couldn't let Gil have it. I'd probably have to hire Kip Dance, and we'd need the money for his wages.

My first thought was that Ma was ignoring what I'd said. I felt a hot flash of anger, just as I'd had so many times when she'd done favors for Gil. I opened my mouth, and if I'd said what I wanted to, I'd have ripped the lid off.

'This is my money,' Ma said before I got a word out. 'There's $104.21. It isn't much, Gil, but it's all I've got, so make it last.'

She handed the money to him and he put it into his pocket, giving her that big smile he had when everything was fine as silk for him. 'Thanks, Ma. I'll bring it back with interest. You'll see.' He kissed her and shook hands with me. 'Good luck, Dave,' he said as if I were the one needing the luck instead of him. 'I'll be back next summer. Probably before roundup. You'll need a hand then.'

He stepped into the saddle, lifted his hat to Ma with a grand flourish, and went down the lane on a dead run. He'll never change, I thought. I looked at my mother. She had her eyes closed; her hands were clasped over her breasts; and her lips were working. She was praying for Gil!

He'd need her prayers, I told myself; he'd need the hand of the Lord right on his shoulder to keep him from starving to death. He'd blow Ma's money before he ever got out of Buhl.

Ma turned and walked into the house. This was the first time she'd been separated from Gil since he'd been born except for a few days at roundup or when we drove the pool herd to the railroad at Rock Springs. It would hit her hard, of course, and I was surprised she hadn't begged him to stay home.

I stood there watching Gil as long as I could see him. As soon as he reached the country road, he turned left and pulled his sorrel down to a slower pace. I started toward the barn, filled with a sudden hot burst of rebellion. Gil could ride off and see the world, but I was the steady one who would stay home and keep the Big Ten going and take care of Ma.

Then the rebellion was gone. Actually I didn't want to see the world. If I'd had my druthers, this was the choice I'd have made.

Kitsy would be home in the summer and everything would be different then. She'd be eighteen. She'd be free of Bess. I'd build another cabin so she wouldn't have to live with Ma. We'd have the life we wanted. I was honest enough to admit that I hoped Gil never came back. I'd be better off without him, even if I had to hire Kip Dance.

My father had said Gil wasn't the kind who'd appreciate a ranch if it were left to him. So the Big Ten was mine. Gil forfeited any right he had by riding off the way he had. Everything would work out, I thought, just the way I wanted it. All I needed was time; all I had to do was wait.

Later in the morning Frank Dance rode over and told me there was going to be a meeting that night in the school-house. I didn't want to go. Everything that was said and done would remind me of my father. That was already happening. The shock of his death was beginning to wear off and now grief was a steady, aching pain from which I could not free myself. But I had to go.

The meeting was different from any I had ever gone to, partly because my father and Gil weren't there, and partly because Bess had nothing to say. I wondered if she were blaming herself for what had happened. Bess was the one who had decided we wouldn't stand for any Rafter 3 cattle wintering in the park. Bess was the one who'd shot a Rafter 3 rider.

Because of that, my father and I had gone to town and Runyan's man Mort had been killed and Sammy Blue wounded.

And there was this business of Bess and Vic Toll. I didn't know what it meant. I couldn't even guess, but I didn't like it. Maybe Bess was selling us out.

So I sat there, listening to the wrangling and feeling sorry for Elder Smith, who had more trouble keeping order than I'd ever known him to have. Presently I was aware of something that bothered me. They were afraid, all of them except Bess and Elder Smith. Fear, my father had often said, was more contagious than smallpox, and now I realized the truth of what he'd said.

They talked about raiding the Rafter 3 and running the crew out of Colorado, about throwing a fence between us and Rafter 3, about building a brush pile on the shoulder of Campbell Mountain and setting fire to it if Toll's men raided us so everyone in the park would be warned. They even talked about hiring a rider to patrol the line between us and the Rafter 3 so he could be a kind of Paul Revere and tell us an attack was on the way.

Finally Matt Colohan got up and said right out what I figured most of them were thinking. 'I've got a wife and houseful of kids. I ain't much of a provider, but I'm better'n nothing. If I got what Joe Munro got, my wife would be in a hell of a fix. Why don't we see how much

Runyan will pay us and go somewhere else?'

Bess couldn't stand that. She got up, her big hands gripping the desk in front of her. 'I'm ashamed of you, Matt. You run now and you'll never stop running. There's a Cameron Runyan on every range.' She swallowed, and then she said, 'We can't betray Joe Munro now. Or Herb Jason, either. My folks are buried close to Joe's grave. I'd rather be right there beside them than go crawling to Runyan.'

Elder Smith said fervently, 'Amen.' After that I couldn't hear anything except our heavy breathing that sounded as if every man in the room had just come in from a long run. Then I couldn't stand it any longer. I heard in my mind the shot that had killed my father; I saw him lying in front of our house.

I got up. I said, 'Matt, if you sell out to Cameron Runyan, I'll kill you. Herb Jason's widow could have got three times the price from Runyan she got from Pa, but she wouldn't take it. What's more, when I find out who killed Pa, I'll take care of him. I'm not going to wait on Ed Veach.'

I sat down. My chin was quivering and my voice wasn't very steady. It wouldn't have taken much to make me burst out bawling. If I had, I'd have sailed into Matt Colohan and beaten him until he'd have wished he'd never opened his mouth.

Elder Smith said: 'Dave's right. We're not

quitting. Matt, let me remind you that your spread isn't the hot spot. If Rafter 3 makes a raid, Dave will be the first to get it, then Bess.'

That was all he needed to say. Somehow he had contrived to make all of them ashamed. Johnny Strong got up and said as much, then moved we adjourn.

Afterward Johnny came to me and shook hands. He said, 'Remember, I told you that you'd have to fill your father's boots. You'll do a pretty good job, I figure.' He gave me a straight look, his face grave. 'Thanks for saying what you did tonight, Dave.'

Frank Dance came to me, too, and shook hands. 'We're as jumpy as a bunch of boogery steers. Everybody's afraid he's gonna get it just like Joe did.' Then he leaned forward and said in a low tone: 'I reckon none of us are gonna wait on Ed Veach, but if you find your man, don't take care of him yourself. A rope's the way to do it, not a bullet.'

CHAPTER EIGHTEEN

The following afternoon Ed Veach showed up in a buggy. I knew the sheriff would have to come and I knew he'd be grumpy. He was. The weather had stayed cold, so the drive across the plateau against the wind must have been anything but pleasant. Add Veach's laziness to

135

the fact that he'd had no love for my father, and catered as much as he could to Cameron Runyan and Vic Toll, and you had more than enough to put him into a towering temper.

When Veach drove into our yard, he looked like an inflated balloon. He was wearing a heavy overcoat, a wool cap with the fur-lined flaps pulled down over his ears, a muffler around his throat and the lower half of his face, and gloves with gauntlets that reached halfway to his elbows. A buffalo robe was spread over his lap.

'Howdy, Munro,' he said. 'A damned cold day.'

'It is,' I agreed. 'Come in and warm up. Stay for supper.'

'No, I'll go on to Elder Smith's place,' Veach said. 'I stopped here to ask you what you know about your pa's death.'

I had given this some thought and made up my mind what to say. I wasn't going to tell him about the footprint I'd found, or that I was convinced the killer lived in the park. Veach wouldn't do anything with the information, except possibly pass it on to Toll and put our man on the run. The way I reasoned, the killer was going to give himself away sooner or later. He must have been paid well, so he'd probably start throwing money around, and then we'd have him.

If I'd had any confidence that the law would function, I'd have felt differently, but with

Veach wearing the star I knew we had to handle this ourselves, so I told Veach how Pa had died and that I'd been sure the saddle tramp Jones had done the killing, and I'd wasted the day chasing him.

Veach listened, but even with his face half covered by the muffler I had the notion he wasn't interested in what I had to say, that he blamed my father for getting himself killed and thereby making Veach drive out here in the cold. When I finished, Veach said, 'I'll have a talk with Colohan before I leave. Thanks, Munro.'

Thanks, Munro! That was all, but it was all I expected. Later I learned he spent two nights with Elder Smith, he did talk to Matt Colohan and went back to Buhl. He made no arrests, he didn't do any more investigating; and when he returned to town he released Jones, who left the country at once.

Our winter was a hard one, the worst Elder Smith could remember. I hired Kip Dance the first of the year, and it was a good thing I did. We had one snowstorm after another. We'd have a warm day or two, then it would turn cold again. Hauling hay and scattering it for our stock was a constant job, one I could not have done by myself.

Kip was good help, good company around the house in the evenings. He slept in Gil's bed, and he never complained about Ma's cooking, and if he was still jealous of me over Kitsy, he didn't show it. He asked about her once in a while because he knew I received at least one letter a week, sometimes two. I told him she seemed to be happy but she wasn't coming home until summer. That satisfied him. I was glad he didn't quiz me about our plans because we didn't have any. All I could do was wait, locked up in the park by the winter as I was, with Kitsy exiled in Denver. Sometimes the waiting was almost more than I could bear.

Bess never told us whether she heard from Gil or not. We didn't, and a cold fury began to grow in me. My mother cried a good deal, not when Kip and I were with her, but I knew she did. Just a postcard from Gil would have satisfied her, a note that he was alive and well. But, no, he couldn't be bothered. Sometimes Ma would put an arm around me and ask, 'Do you think he's all right, Dave?' And I would say, 'Sure he is, Ma. He's just too busy to write.'

Strange, the way it went through those cold, bitter weeks. Because Kip and I almost lived with our cattle, our winter loss was practically nothing: a couple of calves to a wolf; and early in March Kip got the wolf. Even Bess, with two good hands like Barney Lux and Shorty Quinn, had heavier loss than we did, and I heard that Matt Colohan was hard hit. Rafter 3 would be, too. Runyan's cattle were bound to drift, probably as far as White River. A few Rafter 3 steers drifted into the park, and we

138

chased them out. Once we swapped a little lead with Toll's riders, but nobody got hurt.

We were postponing a settlement. I had no idea when it would come, or how, or why Toll didn't strike at us directly; but I had a feeling that the greater the Rafter 3's winter loss was, the bigger price we'd have to pay. I never escaped the feeling that I was living on the edge of a volcano, or that every morning when I stepped out of the door with the milk bucket in my hand I might meet a bullet just as my father had.

I learned a lot of things that winter because I had to. At first I hadn't felt much grief about my father's death. It just didn't seem real. Too, I was half crazy with fury and I kept thinking something would turn up that would point the finger of guilt at the killer, but nothing did. It seemed to me that as the days went by and pushed my father's death farther and farther into the past, I felt his loss more keenly. At times, just looking at some of his things, I would choke up so I couldn't swallow and I'd have to get away by myself. But the thing that surprised me the most, and was the least expected, was the unmistakable fact that my mother and I were being drawn closer together. I'm not sure why. Gil's absence was part of it, but there was something else. I think we began to see in each other characteristics which we hadn't known existed.

She missed Pa, too, and that may have been

part of it. One time in early March she said sadly, 'It's a shame I never realized how much I loved your father when he was alive.'

I told Elder Smith about it one day. He nodded as if that was the way it should be. He said: 'There's nothing as final as death, David. It changes people because it changes life for the living. Your mother sees everything in a different light now than she did when Joe was alive. She knew he would always take care of her no matter what happened, but now you're all she's got.'

Of course there was no way to tell how much Ma had really changed until Gil got back. And he would come back. I never doubted it. He did, late in March. He had been gone three months almost to the day.

I was chopping wood, and Ma was in the henhouse feeding the chickens when I heard her scream, 'Gil! Gil!' I looked up in time to see her drop the bucket of wheat and run across the yard. When I stepped around the corner of the house, I saw him.

If any man ever changed, in appearance at least, Gil had, I doubt if I would have known him if I hadn't recognized his horse. He was that thin. Even with two weeks' growth of beard on his face, his cheeks seemed to have collapsed. His clothes were practically rags. When he dismounted, I saw he wasn't wearing Pa's gun. Even his horse was in bad shape. He'd gone away with all that fanfare, and he'd

140

come home as pathetic a saddle bum as I had ever seen.

Ma kissed him and cried, and I shook hands with him, and so did Kip. He tried to grin, and asked how things were and said the place looked fine and wanted to know had we lost any cattle during the winter. Then he looked at Ma and said, 'Is there anything to eat?'

'Of course, Gil,' she said, and ran into the house.

'I'll take care of your horse,' Kip said, and led the sorrel away.

'Give him a double bait of oats,' Gil called.

I asked, 'Where's Pa's gun?'

I'd been a little sore about him taking it in the first place. He had a good gun of his own, and all I had was that short-barreled monstrosity Pa had bought because it was cheap. I'd naturally figured Pa's gun would be mine, but before I knew what was going on, he'd taken it and left the country.

Gil looked me right in the eyes, not the handsome brother I'd known who'd never had a worry in the world, but a sullen, hungry man who hated me. He said: 'I sold it in Grand Junction to buy something to eat. Go on, cuss me out. Lord it over me. I'm the prodigal son who used up my inheritance in riotous living, and I had to eat with the pigs to even stay alive. Now get out the fatted calf and butcher it. I'm back, Dave. By God, I'm back, and I'm gonna live off the fat of the land like you've been!'

I said, 'Go to the house. Ma'll have supper right away.'

He swung around and went into the kitchen. I finished the wood chopping, needing time for my temper to cool. I kept wondering what Ma would say and do.

When I went into the kitchen with an armload of wood, Gil was at the table eating, wolfishly, as if he were afraid he'd never get his belly full again. Ma was standing beside the stove, staring at him, just filling her eyes with the sight of him. I walked to the sink, and pumped a pan of water, and washed, trying to hold a tight rein on my temper. Kip came in and washed and we sat down and ate.

Gil finally got enough and sat back in his chair and fished the makings out of his pocket. He rolled and lighted his smoke, then he said, 'Well, I went away to see the elephant and I seen him and now I'm back. Just in time for spring work.'

'You won't need me any more, I guess,' Kip said.

'Reckon not,' Gil said. 'Pay him off, Dave.'

I didn't want a showdown in front of Kip, so I got his month's wages. He picked up a few things he had in Gil's room and walked out. I followed him. When he heard me, he turned. 'I'm sorry for you, Dave. Why didn't that bastard get his neck broken?'

'Yeah, why didn't he?' I said. 'Well, you were a good hand, Kip.'

142

'You were a good boss,' he said, and held out his hand. 'So long.'

I shook hands with him. I said, 'Go by Nordine's, will you, and tell Bess he's back.'

He grinned. 'Glad to, Dave.'

I went into the house for the milk bucket. Ma was pumping water and carrying it to the copper boiler that was on the front of the stove. She said, 'Get those clothes off, Gil. They're crawling. I'm going to burn them.'

When I got back, Gil was shaving. He said, 'It'll take me a day or two to see what needs to be done, but looks like you've got things in pretty good shape.'

I carried the milk bucket into the pantry. When I stepped back into the kitchen, I said: 'Let's get something straight, Gil. This spread needs two men to do the work. I guess you're going to be one of them since you wanted to let Kip go, but I've been running the outfit and I'm going to keep on running it. If you need some convincing, we'll step outside and you'll get it.'

Affronted, Gil turned around to look at Ma. 'You going to let him stand there...'

'Gil,' she said, her face showing how miserable she felt, 'things have changed since your father died. Dave's worked hard this winter and he's done well. You'll take his orders if you stay.'

'Well, by God, if that ain't a hell of a note!' He turned back to the mirror on the wall and

143

finished shaving.

Ma found some clean clothes for him, brought in the washtub from the back porch, and filled it with hot water. 'You get in there and scrub up,' she said, and he did, obeying as if he were a small boy.

When he got out of the tub and dressed, I asked, 'Going over to see Bess?'

He whirled to face me. 'No, I'm not going to see Bess. She don't give a damn about me.'

She'd come, all right, but it was another ten minutes before she showed up, crossing the back porch and knocking on the door. I let her in. She barely nodded at me; her eyes on Gil. He stood there, rigid, his hands at his sides. He said, 'How are you, Bess?'

'Oh, Gil, you fool. Don't you know I'm glad to see you?' She ran to him and, folding her arms around him, brought him to her and held him there. 'Don't act that way with me, Gil— not ever. It's enough to have you back.'

I walked out of the house trying to figure it out. Maybe Kitsy could have if she'd been here, but I couldn't.

CHAPTER NINETEEN

This year spring came at once. The grass was up, first in the meadows and pastures that made up the floor of the park, then on the

144

lower slopes of Campbell Mountain. The willows and cottonwoods budded out and the buds burst into leaves; the fruit trees in front of our house were splashes of color. The warm weather held. We'd have a good fruit crop this year unless we got a hailstorm or windstorm later in the season.

Gil and I worked together, and we got along because we had to. He was sullenly silent, sometimes edgy, but I could understand how it was with him. He'd left home with high hopes; but he had returned, whipped and starving, his tail dragging. Through all the years since he had been big enough to be called a man, he had disguised failure so that it looked like success. Now he couldn't do it even to Ma. But he was apparently glad to get three meals a day, to have a bed to sleep in, and to hang around Bess again. He tried to work, and that was all I expected.

Later we did better because we divided the work. Gil spent long days in the saddle with the cattle; I spread manure on the garden and the fields as soon as I could get on the ground, then I plowed. Gil couldn't plow a straight furrow and I could; but he was good with stock, so our division of labor seemed a natural one.

Ma was as busy as Gil and I were. She fussed with her setting hens. She spent hours in the garden as soon as I finished harrowing, breaking up the clods and working the soil with a rake until the garden was like an ashbed. She had an uncanny talent for knowing exactly when to plant each kind of seed, and in a surprisingly short time the radishes, lettuce, and peas broke through the warm, moist ground.

One thing that surprised me was the neutral attitude she took toward Gil. She showed that was she glad he was home, but there was none of the old favoritism that used to make me furious. If Gil expected to be the prodigal son and have the fatted calf butchered for him, he was wrong.

That was the way things were when the peddler, Si Beam, drove into our place one noon. Beam hadn't been in the park since Thanksgiving, when he'd judged the turkey shoot. We were all glad to see him because he brought news from outside, and Ma, in spite of her practical nature, was like a child when she went through the gadgets Beam had to sell.

I helped him put his horse up. I bought a bottle of liniment from him that was, or so he said, good for either man or beast. Then, as we walked across the yard to the house, he said, 'Cameron Runyan's in town this week.'

'Sammy Blue with him?'

'Yeah, he's with the old man,' Beam said. 'He's walking kind o' easy, though.'

'How's his right arm?'

'Stiff. He don't use it. He even eats with his left hand.'

I'd see Blue again, I thought uneasily as I

walked beside Beam. Though we'd lived with a threat of danger ever since Pa was shot, time had blunted the edge. I had expected the assassin to strike again. This might be the time, now that Sammy Blue was back in the country.

We were almost to the back porch when Beam said: 'Dave, I've got a message from Runyan. He paid me money to deliver it. It's for everybody in the park. You suppose we could call a meeting tonight?'

'No. We're too busy.'

He sighed. 'I know you're busy, but this is important. To tell the truth, I can't afford to lose the money he paid me. You know how it was all winter. I didn't get out much with my rig, and damned if I ain't broke.' He looked at me expectantly, but I didn't give him any sympathy. I was just as broke as he was. He said: 'Look, Dave. I can't help it if everybody's too busy to come to a meeting, but I've got to tell Runyan I tried. Trouble is, my say-so ain't enough to get anybody to come. Yours would be, though.'

'I won't get any plowing done by sashaying from one end of the park to the other,' I said irritably.

'I'd pay you five dollars for an afternoon's work. Maybe you could use five dollars.'

I could use it, all right. If I didn't go, somebody else would. By now Runyan would have a report from Vic Toll. From what I'd heard, Rafter 3's winter loss had been bad. To a careful, greedy man like Cameron Runyan, that news would be enough to drive him wild.

If Rafter 3 stock had wintered in the park, the loss would have been negligible. I knew that Runyan had been driven to offer some kind of a deal. I wanted to know what it was, even though I was sure we'd never do business with him.

'Tell you what I'll do, Si,' I said. 'Along with that five dollars, you let Ma pick out any piece of cloth you've got, enough for a dress, and I'll call the meeting.'

'It's a deal,' he said.

When we went into the kitchen and I told Ma about it, she laughed, one of the few times I had ever heard a laugh of sheer pleasure break spontaneously from her. 'Dave, do you know how long it's been since I had a new dress?'

I didn't, but I knew then, just by looking at her, that an afternoon of lost work was a small price to pay for the pleasure a new dress would give her. Funny about that. Ma wouldn't buy the cloth from Si. She'd never bought more than a few gimcracks—a package of needles or pins or maybe a bottle of vanilla extract—but she'd accept any deal I made with Beam as long as it didn't cost money.

I met with a lot of grumbling that afternoon, but all the park ranchers came to the meeting. They felt, just as I did, that we ought to know what Runyan had to offer, even if nothing came of it. It was a good indication of our

148

unity, I thought, especially with travel so difficult. The road was a loblolly in a number of places where it hadn't been graded.

Beam shook hands all around and got right down to business as soon as Elder Smith called the meeting to order. He said: 'First of all, I don't want you folks to think I'm Cameron Runyan's errand boy. I'm a peddler—no more and no less. I've come to Dillon's Park every fall and spring for years. You've all been generous, and there never was a time when I left the park regretting that I came. But the way the roads are, I wouldn't have come this early if it hadn't been for the deal Runyan wants to make. In fact, I hesitated quite a while, but you've been so wonderful to me that I thought I ought to come.'

By that time I was suspicious. Maybe I didn't have any right to be. Si Beam seemed very earnest. He was the one man who could have come to us from Runyan without arousing instant resentment. I think he knew it, but to my way of thinking, he overdid it, with his leathery old face exuding good will. Elder Smith often quoted Shakespeare, something about he protesteth too much, and that was exactly what Beam was doing.

Before he could go on, Frank Dance broke in, 'Si, are you going to tell us what Runyan had to do with Joe Munro's murder?'

Beam froze, his eyes flicking nervously around the room, and for a few seconds a dropped pin would have sounded like a tenpenny nail. Then he said: 'Frank, I respected Joe Munro as much as the next man. If I knew anything about his murder, anything at all, I'd have gone to Ed Veach a long time ago.'

'A lot of good that'd do,' Johnny Strong grumbled.

'True, but he's the sheriff and we're the voters and we put him into office,' Beam said. 'Now let's get on with our business. Remember, I'm not trying to persuade you to take Runyan's offer. I'm just fetching it to you. If you're wondering why he's making it, I think I can tell you. Rafter 3's loss this winter was terrible. Some of their stock drifted to hellan'gone, and nobody knows when they'll get it all back. I doubt if they know themselves how bad the loss is. Runyan's going to be in town for another week—'

'Si,' Bess interrupted, her voice sharp with impatience, 'if Runyan wants to buy us out, the answer's No, just like it always has been.'

Beam stopped and licked his lips, plainly disconcerted. He took a folded sheet of paper out of his coat pocket and opened it. He said, 'He wants to buy, all right, but this time he's making a definite offer for each ranch.'

We sat there listening against our will simply because none of us would get up and kick Si Beam out the door. He reeled off the figures: $7,000 for the Big Ten, $15,000 for Anchor,

$12,000 for Dance's Diamond 8, $6,000 for Matt Colohan's Bar M. They sounded like big prices, I suppose. $5,000 profit on the Big Ten was fantastic, but there was a joker in the deck. Cattle prices were up since Pa bought the outfit and the ranch was in the best shape it ever had been. Both Bess and Frank Dance had told me that. I glanced at Gil, and he grinned and shook his head and I knew that for once we agreed on something.

When Beam finished, Elder Smith said quietly, 'Cameron Runyan seems to be a persistent man. Tell him the answer is still no.'

But the weak link in our chain was Matt Colohan. He was the only rancher in the park who had suffered severe winter loss, and to him $6,000 must have sounded like a million. After listening to the prices Runyan was offering, it seemed to me that the only one which was out of line was for Colohan's Bar M: $6,000 was too much. Runyan might not have realized the shape Matt's spread was in; but on the other hand, he may have known Colohan was the man to work on.

I sat across the aisle from Colohan; I saw his face get red and his chin begin to quiver. He had his tail in a crack, all right, wanting to sell but scared to say so. Finally he jumped up. He shouted, 'By God, all of you can say No till you run out of spit, but I'm gonna take Runyan's price and get to hell out of here!'

Frank Dance stood up and, grabbing

151

Colohan by the shoulder, whirled him around and hit him. The sound of the blow was a meaty thud that could have been heard anywhere in the room. Dance was a powerful man, and I don't think he intended to hit Colohan as hard as he did. But whether he did or not, Colohan went down and lay still, knocked cold.

Dance rubbed his knuckles against his shirt. 'Sorry Matt can't hear what I've got to say, but somebody can tell him. I'll kill the first man who sells out to Runyan. I've heard Johnny Strong say the same thing in this room. I've heard Dave Munro say it. Now I say it. Joe Munro died for something, and I ain't gonna let his death go to waste.'

Dance jerked his head at Kip and they walked out. I got up and looked down at Colohan, who still hadn't moved. I said: 'We're going to hang and rattle, but there's one thing we can count on. We'll hear from Runyan after Si goes back to town and tells him our answer. Pa's murderer is still around.'

'Makes no never mind,' Johnny Strong said. 'We've got to stand solid or we won't be standing at all.'

We broke up a few minutes after that; Si Beam not very happy about the way it had gone. He left the park the next day, not making the rounds as he had always done before.

Three days later Kip Dance rode in on a dead run just as I finished milking. He reined up and stared down at me, tears running down his cheeks. He wiped his face with his sleeve and tried to say something but choked up, then got it out. 'Elder Smith was shot and killed this morning. Just like your pa. He went out through his back door, same as he always does 'bout sunup, and he got it in the brisket.'

CHAPTER TWENTY

We buried Elder Smith on a warm afternoon, spring a feeling and a smell in the air. From somewhere over in Frank Dance's field a meadowlark added its sweet tone to our hymns. Above us a hawk glided noiselessly through the air. The earth, still moist from the snow that had gone off several weeks ago, was soft underfoot, and the entire cemetery, with the exception of my father's grave, was green with grass where only a few weeks before it had been a drab brown.

Afterwards, when I was riding home with Kip and his father, I asked, 'You didn't pick up any sign at all?'

I had asked it before, but I couldn't help thinking that maybe Frank was holding something back just as I had when my father was killed. Frank shook his head. 'I found some cigarette stubs back of the store, and a horse had been left in the shed behind the schoolhouse, maybe for a couple of hours; but no tracks. You know how hard that ground is: packed down like a floor.'

We had nothing to go on then, less even than I knew about my father's killer. I said, 'I guess I should have told you before, Frank, but I think the man we want lives here in the park.'

Kip said, 'The hell!'

Frank nodded, tight-lipped. 'I figure the same, Dave. Whoever done it must have known Joe's and the Elder's habits. Joe always went out the front door to milk. The Elder always got up before sunup and went out the back, rain or shine, winter or summer. He was never one to lay in bed. Had to see the sun come up.' Frank shook his head at me. 'What does that tell us?'

'One thing's damned sure,' Kip said. 'If we'd taken Runyan's offer the other night, Elder Smith would be alive.'

'I ain't sure about that, Kip,' Frank said. 'Maybe Runyan gave the order. Maybe Toll did it, thinking that was what his boss wanted. But then again, maybe it was the same bastard who killed Joe, figuring the job was good for another chunk of dinero. What I'm saying, is we can't go off half cocked. Not yet.'

We rode in silence until we reached their lane, when Frank said: 'Don't tell anybody what we're thinking, Dave. Not even Gil or your mother.'

'I won't,' I said, and rode on.

We had church the following Sunday morning, of a sort. Bess refused to take charge because she said it was no job for a woman. Finally Frank Dance walked up to the front of the room. He made a ludicrous figure standing beside the organ, red in the face, the Bible almost lost in his great hands, his deep voice expressionless as he stated each word as if it were an entire sentence and had no connection with the next one. His wide shoulders were constantly trying to break through the coat of his store suit, but he tried, and we all gave him credit for that.

After the service was over we lingered outside. The day was a warm one with a few lacy white clouds caressing the top of Campbell Mountain. No one seemed to want to go home. Fear was with us. There was no mistaking it. Not that it was really voiced in words, but every one of us, I was sure, was asking himself the obvious question: Who would be next?

There were plans to make if we were to go on living here. Bess said she'd teach school next fall if we couldn't find anyone. Lorna Dance agreed to come over and keep the store open in the afternoons and work the mail that came in from Buhl twice a week.

Then Matt Colohan couldn't control himself any longer. He shouted: 'You're a bunch of fools! We had a chance to sell at a good price and get out of the park, but you wouldn't let me do it.'

'Shut up, Matt,' Johnny Strong said. 'Shut that up.'

But now that it was started, he couldn't shut up. 'I'm gonna talk,' Matt shouted. 'It's past time to talk. We've had two killings. They can go right on smoking us down one at a time, and what can we do if we don't get out? Tell me that, Johnny, if you're so smart!'

But Johnny had no answer. He looked at his wife who was holding her baby in her arms, and she looked at him, but neither said a word. I glanced at Riley MacKay. His gaze was on his wife. She was the city girl who'd leave Riley, folks said; but now she was holding her shoulders high and proud and she was the one who answered Matt.

'We're not smart, Matt,' she said. 'Not any of us. None of us wants to die, either, but we're going to stay because our homes are here.'

You never knew about a person, I thought, not what was inside until the squeeze was on. Mrs. Riley MacKay would be all right, and the gossips like Mrs. Colohan would stop talking about her. She'd stay with Riley and make her home here and raise her children. Yes, she'd be all right, and even Matt was ashamed.

'Yeah, reckon we'll stay,' he muttered.

Then Gil said: 'If Dave wasn't such a stupid fool, Elder Smith would be alive today.'

We looked at him. We stopped breathing, I guess. I know I did. It was the same as if we had been shocked by a sudden downpour of cold water. He didn't look at me. He stood beside my mother, about ten feet from me, his face grave, his gaze moving from Frank Dance to Johnny Strong and on to Luke Jordan. Then a fire got hold of me and I began to tremble.

For me, at that moment, everyone disappeared except Gil. Frank Dance's voice, a heavy bass, barely reached my ears, 'What do you mean, Gil?'

'Why, he had to do everything himself when Pa was killed,' Gil said. 'Didn't even stay to help get Pa's body inside. Just grabbed his gun and saddled up and spent all day hunting that saddle tramp Jones. While he was doing that, the killer got away, the same killer who shot Elder Smith.'

Little red lights started dancing in front of my eyes. In that one instant all the injustices I'd suffered at Gil's hands, the slights, the extra work I'd had to do, the whippings he'd given me when I was too small to have any show against him: all of it boiled up in memory and roared through my mind like an exploding sky rocket.

I took two long strides and hit him, my fist coming up from my boot tops. Maybe he didn't see it coming. Maybe he wanted me to hit him. I don't really know, but he didn't duck or try to ward off my blow. I caught him square on the chin, and he went back and down, knocked as cold as Frank Dance had knocked

Matt Colohan the night of the meeting when Si Beam was here.

A woman screamed. Another one cried, 'He's killed him!'

My mother was on her knees, cradling Gil's head in her lap. She looked up at me, and I saw hate in her eyes, or I thought I did, hate that must have gone back through all the years when she was raising us, or back maybe to the moment I was conceived.

She said: 'Go away, Dave. Never come back. I don't want to see you again.'

I couldn't move for a time. I just stood staring at her while my world and my dreams came tumbling down on top of me. The Big Ten wouldn't be mine. I couldn't marry Kitsy. I wouldn't have any place to bring her, any way to make a living for her.

I wheeled and ran toward my horse. I felt a hand on my arm—Johnny Strong's, I think— but I jerked free and kept on. I mounted and rode away, my horse kicking up the soft dirt of the road as he ran. I didn't look back, and I couldn't look ahead.

CHAPTER TWENTY-ONE

When I reached our house, I left my horse beside the back porch, the reins dragging, and ran inside. I wasn't thinking coherently. I guess

I wasn't thinking at all. I buckled my gun belt around me and picked up my father's Winchester. Gil wasn't going to sell it. I got my twelve dollars out of the bureau drawer, found a flour sack in the pantry and filled it with food, including a ham Ma had baked a day or two before. When I went outside, Bess was waiting for me.

I tied the sack behind the saddle, not wanting to talk to Bess. All I wanted was to get out of there. She said, 'What are you going to do, Dave?'

'I don't know.'

'You're making a mistake,' she said. 'You're acting like a kid.'

'Then I'm acting like Gil.'

'That's right.'

I stood looking at her. At that moment I hated her the same way I hated Gil and Ma. Right then I hated everybody. 'Get out of my way, Bess. Don't argue with me. By God, I'm leaving!'

Instead of getting out of my way, she grabbed the reins of my horse. 'You're so mad you don't know what you're doing. Now you stand there until you cool off. There's something I want you to do.'

'I'm cooled off. What do you want?'

'I want you to help me find your father's killer.'

That did cool me off. I said, 'If I knew how to do that—'

'I think I know, but you have to realize you've got to come home after you do what I want you to. Your mother will be awfully sorry about what she said. I think she'll tell you she is. As far as Gil's concerned, he got what was coming to him. Dave, I don't know what's the matter with him. I'm going to marry him. I told him I would the other night, but...'

She stopped and stared at the ground, scraping her foot back and forth across the dirt. 'I guess. I do know what's wrong with him. I just don't want to admit it. He went away because I asked him to. He made a lot of big promises and he didn't keep one of them. He came back broke and half-starved. His pride was hurt. Today he was trying to pull you down to his level, I guess. He's jealous of you. He'd like to be more like you, and Dave, I think you'd like to be more like him.'

'The hell I do,' I shouted.

She shrugged. 'I didn't come here to argue. I'm trying to say that if you're gone a little while, you'll have your mother and Gil awfully glad to see you when you get back. I want you to get a job with Vic Toll.'

That knocked the wind out of me. All I could do was just stand there and stare at her. I had always figured Bess Nordine was an intelligent woman with more than her share of horse sense. But for me to ask Vic Toll for a job wasn't any kind of sense.

She must have seen how it hit me. She said:

'Now wait before you blow up. The man we want lives in the park. I thought that when your father was shot. After Elder Smith was killed the same way, I was sure of it. If I'm right, Toll will hear about what happened today. He'll think you're so sore at Gil and your mother and the rest that he can use you, and you've got to fix it so he can.'

'Hell,' I said in disgust. 'If I rode into Rafter 3, they'd smoke me out of my saddle before I could say a word!'

'Don't do it that way. You know the old Harris cabin?' I nodded, and she went on: 'You hole up there for a while. It hasn't been used for a long time, so it's probably dirty, but you can make out. It'll be dangerous because it's on Rafter 3 range, so you'll have to be careful, but if you handle it right, I think you'll be safe. Sooner or later they'll come around to see who's there. You tell them you're finished in the park and you're hanging around waiting for a chance to get square for us blaming you for not getting your father's killer. Toll will believe you because that's the way he thinks. Take my word for it, Dave. I *know*.'

She looked at the ground again, biting her lip. It hurt her, I thought, to say even that much about Toll, so I waited. A moment later she went on: 'You'll just have to play it by ear. If you see Toll, lay it on thick. If you don't see him, feel out whoever you're talking to about getting a job. Spring round-up will start pretty

161

soon. Toll always needs more men; I think he'll take you on. Then you'll just have to watch. Maybe you'll have to trail him. If he catches you at it, he'll kill you, so be careful. Or our man may try to see him. Some of his crew might talk. I don't know what will happen, but something will. You may not bring back any proof, but if I know who to go after, I'll get the proof.'

'All right, I'll try it,' I said, and taking the reins from her, stepped into the saddle. I didn't really care. I didn't care about anything right then.

'I'll bring some grub to you in a couple of days,' she said. 'Probably after dark.' She laid a hand on my leg. 'Dave, don't get yourself killed. I'd never forgive myself if that happened. But this will go on until we stop it, and I want to stop it now. I'm the next in line.' She stepped back. 'I'm asking you to save my life. I guess that's what it amounts to.'

That surprised me more than anything else she'd said. She was as scared as anyone else except Matt Colohan.

'Maybe you're the one who'd better be careful,' I said, and rode away.

*　　　*　　　*

The Harris cabin had been built by a bachelor long before we came to the park. It was in better shape than I had expected. Pack rats had been all over it, but there was a broom inside, so I was able to get it cleaned up reasonably well. The walls and roof were tight, the door and windows intact, and there was some furniture that was usable: a stove, table, bunk, and a couple of chairs.

Probably the Rafter 3 hands used it occasionally. I was fairly sure some of them would make a swing out this way and get close enough to see smoke coming out of the chimney. I found an old rusty ax back of the cabin, so I chopped up a dead cedar, built a fire, and cooked supper. After that I settled down to wait, and wait I did for two days.

They were the longest days of my life. I discovered I wasn't cut out to be a hermit. I sat in front of the cabin and stared at the land that reached from my ridge to the horizon, all Rafter 3 range: an ocean of sagebrush and greasewood, with here and there dark patches of cedar, and winding through it like a looped green string was Buck Creek, bordered by willows and cottonwoods. Ridges and arroyos, with an occasional finger of rock lifting maybe a hundred feet above the plateau.

Bess came as she had promised, after dark. She gave me a sack of grub, but she wouldn't get down. 'Somebody might be watching, might even have trailed me. I just wanted to tell you I've talked to your mother and she's sorry she said what she did. She wants you back, Dave.'

I didn't say anything. I stood looking up at Bess in the moonlight, sour-tempered because she'd brought up something I didn't want to think about. She went on: 'I curried Gil down. If he wasn't sorry before, he is now.' She laughed softly. 'For one thing, he doesn't like to milk.'

I said, 'Nothing's happened, Bess.'

'They'll come,' she said. 'Dave, you've got enough bitterness in you to destroy you if you let it.'

'I'll wait a little longer,' I said. 'So long.'

She sighed. 'I'll be back to see you in two or three days,' she said, and rode away.

The thing worked out, but not in the way Bess expected it to. The next afternoon two Rafter 3 riders showed up. I saw them coming a long time before they reached the cabin. They'd drop out of sight into an arroyo and then show up again on a ridge, zigzagging a little but generally heading toward the cabin.

I checked my revolver and slipped it back into the holster. I left the Winchester just inside the door and stood in front of the cabin until the two riders came out of a bunch of cedars below me and started up the slope. Then I retreated one step so I stood in the doorway where I could grab the rifle if I wanted it, or jump back inside. I had to consider the possibility there were others, maybe circling above me; although I doubted it because there was a kind of arrogant confidence in all Rafter

3 hands. They believed that two of them could more than handle any man whether he was Billy the Kid or some of the Wild Bunch.

I recognized them when they reined up: Dick Price and Slim Jim. I didn't know how they got their names or where they came from or anything about them. They were just a pair of Rafter 3 cowhands who had come to the park the previous spring to gather Rafter 3 stock that had wintered there.

They recognized me too, which surprised me because they'd had nothing to do with me. Price said: 'Well, I'll be damned! Look who we've got here, Slim.'

'Yeah, it's the Gunslick Kid,' Slim Jim said. 'Busted Sammy Blue's arm. Remember, Dick?'

Price laughed. 'I heerd about it. Sammy remembers. I'll bet on that.'

'If you're looking for trouble,' I said, 'you can have it.'

'I'm not,' Price said. 'I'll let Blue stomp his own snakes.'

'What are you doing on Rafter 3 range?' Slim asked.

'I quit the park,' I said. 'Didn't you hear about it?'

'Yeah, seems like I did, now that you mention it,' Price admitted. 'Had a tussle with your brother, and your ma told you to hit a high lope out of there. That right?'

They had a grapevine into the park, all right. I asked, 'How'd you hear?'

Slim Jim grinned. 'You hear a lot of things, kid, listening to the leaves rustle, but you ain't told us what you're doing here. If you're figuring on taking up a homestead, you're a goner.'

'Me homestead?' I laughed. 'Hell, no! I just had to have some place to hole up and this was handy. I've been so God-damned mad I didn't know what to do. Been figuring on going back and having it out with Gil.'

'He handles a gun purty fancy, don't he?' Price asked.

'That's why I haven't gone back,' I said. 'Say, you reckon I could get a job with the Rafter 3?'

'You serious?' Price asked incredulously.

'You bet I am,' I said. 'I can't keep living off hot air. I've got to get a job somewhere, and I'd rather hang around here and see what happens in the park.' I kicked at the door casing. 'Gil never did any good for that park bunch. I have. I set Gil on his butt and Ma told me where I could go. Do any of them offer me a place to stay? Johnny Strong or Frank Dance or any of them? No, sir! I can go to hell for all they care.'

Price scratched his long nose and glanced at Slim Jim. 'Sounds like he means it.'

'Can't blame him none,' Slim Jim said. 'A scummy lot down there. Purely scummy.' He looked at me. 'Vic's in Rock Springs. I'll tell him about you.'

Price glanced at Slim Jim again, slyly, I

thought, then brought his gaze to me. He said, 'You hang around here, will you, Munro? I'll ride over and tell you when Vic gets back.'

'I'll be here,' I said. 'Long as my grub holds out, anyway.'

They rode away. I watched them for a long time until they disappeared out there in that maze of gullies and ridges. They had something up their sleeves, all right, but I couldn't figure it out. They hadn't threatened me, hadn't tried to run me off. All they wanted was to pin me down, but I didn't have the slightest idea why.

I found out the following day. A rider showed up about the middle of the afternoon, coming in the same way Dick Price and Slim Jim had come the day before. I didn't recognize him until he reached the bottom of the ridge below the cabin, and when I did, I wished I was somewhere else.

It was Sammy Blue!

CHAPTER TWENTY-TWO

Blue rode up the slope toward the cabin, his eyes on me. He held the reins in his left hand; his right arm hung at his side. I stood in the doorway, thinking that I could shoot him out of his saddle without running any chance of getting shot. But I didn't try. I guess he knew I wouldn't.

He dismounted and walked toward me, his right arm still hanging at his side. His gun was on his left hip. I remembered what the saddle tramp Jones had said about Blue when he'd seen him in Rock Springs. His right arm was stiff! That was the way it looked now. And I was remembering what Vic Toll had said. Sammy Blue was as good with his left hand as he had been with his right. But was he? Well, I'd soon find out.

As Blue walked toward me, I backed up. By the time he reached the doorway, I was standing against the opposite wall of the cabin. He stopped, a little bandy-legged man, his left hand close to the butt of his gun. He was silhouetted against the light so that his face was in the shadow and I couldn't see his expression, but it seemed to me I could feel his hate, almost as if it were an odor rushing across the cabin to me.

At times I suppose all of us have a weird feeling that here is a moment we have lived before, perhaps in some other life and in other circumstances. That was exactly the way I felt at that moment, but oddly enough, I didn't know how it had turned out before. I only knew that if Sammy Blue was as good with his left hand as he had been with his right, I was a dead man. Bess Nordine would regret she had sent me here, but her regret wasn't going to save me.

'I'm going to kill you, Munro,' Blue said. 'I

guess you know that.'

I hoped he would make his play then, because the interior of the cabin was dark compared to the bright sunlight he had been used to, and he might have trouble seeing me. I wanted to start the ball myself, but I had never drawn a gun against a man when I was facing him, and I couldn't quite bring myself to do it now. I had no confidence that I could match the speed of Blue's draw, so I was looking death squarely in the face, and I felt a frantic desire to live. In the back of my mind, I suppose, there was a small hope that something would happen to stop this, that time was on my side, but if I started the fight, I wasn't giving time a chance to work.

Blue seemed to be in no hurry. He stood motionless, staring at me, maybe waiting for his eyes to become accustomed to the thin light. Or perhaps this was his way, enjoying the cat-and-mouse game he had played with my father last fall in the lobby of the hotel in Buhl.

'I had quite a ride,' he said finally. 'I was in town, or I'd have been here sooner. Price rode in to get me.' He lifted his right arm a few inches and dropped it back to his side. 'You didn't think I'd forget you did this to me, did you?'

I didn't answer. Suddenly I knew why I'd had that weird feeling of having lived through this moment before. It wasn't from any other life. I didn't have to accept any strange

169

explanation like that. Sammy Blue was right. Right from the moment I'd shot him in Buhl, I'd know I'd have to face him again. Suddenly frantic desire to live clawed through my consciousness and I thought of Kitsy and what it would mean to her if I died this way.

'You're scared, sonny,' Blue said. 'You're scared right down to your guts. You can't move and you can't talk.'

I *had* been scared; then suddenly I wasn't. I wouldn't beg and I wouldn't crawl. I had forgotten for a moment, but now I remembered that he had sent the saddle tramp Jones to Dillon's Park.

'I can talk,' I said. 'You're no gun fighter. You're a God-damned bushwacker. You murdered my father.'

He was surprised at that. He said: 'I didn't kill Joe.'

'Then who did?'

'Barney Lux,' Blue said, and grinned. 'And he killed Elder Smith too. Surprised?'

I was surprised, all right, but I tried not to show it. I couldn't afford to let my mind release the attention I had fixed on the gunman. I had to move the instant he did.

'Five hundred dollars for each job,' Blue said, 'but that's his way, not mine. I work for Runyan. Barney worked for Toll.'

He couldn't stand it any longer. I suppose he'd been using up time so that fear would work on me, and he thought he had waited long enough. He made his play with his left hand and I made mine.

I never made a smoother, faster draw, maybe because I knew I had to, and of course I had the advantage of the short barrel. I was way ahead of Blue. He didn't get off a shot. My first bullet caught him in the left shoulder and knocked him back out of the doorway as cleanly as if he had been jerked off his feet by an invisible wire. I fired again as he fell, the bullet angling through his chest.

I ran out of the cabin and stood over him. His eyes were open, and blood was bubbling out of his mouth and running down his chin. I thought I saw shock in that little squeezed-up face of his, the kind of shock that comes to a man when he believes he holds a pat hand and discovers he hasn't when it's too late.

'I practiced but not enough,' he said.

He spoke slowly, whispering the words, for that was all the strength he had. Then he was dead, his mouth dropping open, his hands going slack in the dust at his sides. I leaned against the cabin wall for a time, my knees weak, blood pounding through my body. All the practicing he'd done with his left hand had not been enough. Maybe he'd thought he was ready. Or maybe he knew he'd fail, but still he'd had to try when Dick Price told him where I was.

I dropped my gun back into holster and dragged Blue's body inside the cabin.

Somebody would come after him when he didn't show up at the Rafter 3. I jerked the bridle off his horse and gave him a slap. I got my Winchester from the cabin and shut the door, then saddled up and started for the park. I'd tell Bess, and then I'd take care of Barney Lux.

By the time I reached the park, the sun had been down by two hours and the moon was up. I'd been thinking about what I should do from the moment I'd left the cabin. My mind had never worked more clearly than it did on that ride. I decided the best help I could get for the job ahead was Frank Dance.

When I got to his place, Frank was in bed asleep, but in no time at all he and Kip had saddled up and were riding with me to Bess's house.

We rode most of the way up the lane to Bess's house, then we stopped. We could see a light in the house, but not in the bunkhouse. I said, 'Bess is up, but chances are Lux is asleep. How about walking in and letting Kip hold the horses here?'

I had a look at Frank's big square face, but I couldn't tell much in the moonlight. After a moment's thought, he said, 'All right. Be a sight easier if we catch the bastard asleep.'

We dismounted and walked to the house, moving quietly and saying nothing. I knocked on the front door, Frank standing a step behind me. When the door opened, Bess saw who it was and, turning, said, 'Gil, Dave's back.'

I wished to hell he was ten miles from there. Now we were stuck with him. He got up from his chair and walked to the door. He was nervous and red in the face. I thought at first he was afraid I intended to tie into him again, but it wasn't that.

'I'm apologizing for what I said last Sunday.' He held out his hand. 'I'm sorry. You done right to take a poke at me.'

I took his hand, so surprised that I found it hard to believe this was actually happening. He had never apologized to anyone as far as I knew, but to apologize to me of all people was something that came under the heading of a miracle.

'It's all right, Gil,' I said. 'Forget it.'

'You'll come home?'

'It's up to Ma.'

'All right.'

I wasn't going to waste time making up with Gil. First I had to tell Bess about Barney Lux; then Frank and I were going to root him out of the bunkhouse.

CHAPTER TWENTY-THREE

Gil wouldn't have gone to the bunkhouse with us if Bess hadn't motioned for him to go. As it was, he hung back. When we were outside, Frank Dance said, 'How're we gonna do this?'

'We'll open the door and go barreling in,' I said. 'If he's got a gun in bed with him, and tries to use it, we'll drill him right there.'

'No,' Frank said. 'He's gonna hang.'

He was right, of course. My quick answer showed how trigger jumpy I was. We stood there in the moonlight looking at each other, all three of us uncertain. Finally Gil said, 'Barney's got the bunk next to the door. There's a bull's eye lantern hanging on the back porch. If we go in fast and put the lantern right on him, we'll have him before he knows what's up.'

'How about Shorty?' Frank asked.

'He won't give us any trouble,' I said.

'All right,' Frank said. 'We'll try it.'

We swung around the house to the back porch, lighted the lantern, and moved on to the bunkhouse, making as little noise as possible. When we reached the door, Frank whispered: 'You open up, Gil. I'll hold the lantern. Dave, keep your gun on him but don't shoot.'

We went in fast just as we planned, the light beam on Lux, who sat up in bed, scowling and blinking, too shocked to even try for his gun. I reached the side of his bunk in about three jumps, jerked his covers back, and rammed my gun into his gut.

'You're under arrest for the murder of Pa and Elder Smith,' I said. 'Get out of bed and

174

dress!'

Shorty Quinn made a dive across the bunkhouse for his Winchester. I didn't think he'd try for it, but I suppose any man would have, jarred out of a deep sleep by three men breaking into the bunkhouse and not knowing who they were or why they were there. Frank called: 'Stay out of it, Shorty! We don't want you.' Quinn had a hand on his rifle, then he dropped it and stood staring at us.

Lux surprised me more than Shorty. He looked at me, then at Frank, who was a step behind me holding the lantern, and finally at Gil, who was back by the door. Then he asked, 'Did that bastard of a Vic Toll tell you I done it?'

'Makes you no never mind who told,' I said. 'We know you were paid $500 for each killing. Toll got a bargain.'

My gun muzzle was still deep in his belly. He was afraid to move, I guess, but he didn't cave. His beady little eyes were bright in the lantern light. He didn't seem to be afraid, probably because he thought we were taking him to jail and he was confident Vic Toll would get him off. He said, 'Sounds like you got good information.'

'Back up, Dave,' Frank said. 'Let him dress.'

So I backed up, holding the gun on him while he dressed. When we left the bunkhouse, Shorty was still standing a step away from his Winchester. Frank said: 'Shorty, in case you're

175

asked, you don't know nothing 'bout this. Savvy?'

'I savvy, all right,' Shorty said.

Gil shut the door behind us. When we got to the front of the house, Frank called, 'Kip, fetch the horses in.'

We went into the house, Frank blowing out the lantern and putting it down just inside the door. Bess was sitting where we had left her. Kitsy was a good housekeeper, and when she'd been home the place was always in order; but now it was cluttered with newspapers, magazines, catalogues, and all kinds of odds and ends. You'd have thought it was a man's place.

When we came in, Bess jumped up and cleared off the leather couch, throwing an armload of stuff into a corner of the room. 'Frank, you and Gil sit here.' She pulled a raw-hide-bottom chair into the middle of the room. 'Barney, this is yours.' She drew a chair up to the walnut stand and sat down. 'You're the prosecutor, Dave, so you'll stand up. We'll wait till Kip comes in.'

Lux still wasn't worried. He sat down, a smug grin on his heavy-lipped mouth. 'What the hell is the fuss about, Bess? Why don't we start for town?'

'We're not going to town,' Bess said. 'You're going to be tried right here by this court.'

'Court?' Lux jeered. 'What kind of a kangaroo layout do you call this? Any man's

176

got a right to a trial.'

Bess gripped the sides of the stand and leaned forward. She said: 'Barney, you've worked for Anchor for a long time. I suppose you've been taking Rafter 3 pay right along. A lot of things are clear now. Toll aways knew what was going on in the park. You never went to church or anywhere else, but maybe you figured that would keep us from suspecting you. It worked with me. I should have seen through you but I didn't.'

'You just said I didn't go to nothing,' Lux muttered. 'How do you figure I could tell Toll anything?'

'Because I trusted you,' Bess snapped. 'I talked in front of you about everything that went on. Kitsy did too, when she was home. So did Shorty. All you had to do was listen.'

Lux was a good listener, I thought. He was a silent man, and Bess, who was used to him, had accepted it as his way and never given it a thought. Neither had Shorty. They were the two people in the park who were with Lux most of the time and got along with him because they had to.

Now Bess, who had never wanted to admit a mistake, was forced to admit to herself that she had been wrong in trusting Barney Lux, and so had inadvertently helped bring about the death of my father and Elder Smith. It seemed to me that must be what she was thinking. At least her thoughts were far from pleasant. One look

177

at her face was enough to tell me that.

When Kip came in, Bess motioned for him to sit down beside Gil and Frank. She said, 'We're a self-constituted court. I guess we're all aware that we may suffer for what we do tonight, but we've got to do it.' We nodded agreement, and she looked at Lux. 'You are accused of the murder of Joe Munro and Elder Smith. Do you plead guilty or not guilty?'

Lux acted as if he had suddenly awakened to the fact that we were determined to carry this through to the end. He said, 'By God, I ain't standing for no more of this hoorawing! I'll take my time and get to hell out of here!'

He got up and glared at Bess. I had holstered my gun, but now I lifted it from leather and lined it on his middle. 'Sit down,' I said, 'or you won't live long enough to taste a rope.'

He sat down, muttering something under his breath. Bess asked, 'How do you plead?'

'I ain't pleading nothing,' Lux said. 'This ain't a court. Nothing you can do or say will make it a court.'

Bess nodded at me. 'What's your evidence against him, Dave?'

'I've got a question to ask first,' I said. 'Where was he the days Pa and Elder Smith were killed?'

'I've been thinking about that,' Bess said. 'He told me he wanted to go to town Christmas and turn his wolf loose. He never had before. He was gone two days, Christmas day and the

178

next day, and when he got back he said he'd been in a fight and got drunk and stayed in town. I asked Ed Veach about it when he was here, and he didn't know anything about a fight. I should have known then.'

'What about the day Elder Smith was killed?' I asked.

'He was gone then, too. He went up to our line cabin on Campbell Mountain. At least, that's what he said. Needed cleaning up, he told me. We'll be putting a man up there in a few days, so I let him go.'

I said: 'Before I left the morning Pa was shot, I looked around. I found some cigarette stubs. Barney smokes cigarettes. I did find one good bootheel track in the snow. It looked like a new boot.'

'Barney bought a pair early in December,' Bess said.

'Sammy Blue told me it was Barney,' I said. 'He claimed Barney worked for Toll, not Runyan, and that he got $500 for each killing. When we got him out of bed just now, I told him that and he said we had good information.'

'Anything else?' Bess asked.

'Not from me,' I said, 'but Frank told me he found cigarette stubs back of the store the morning Elder Smith was killed.'

'That's right,' Frank agreed. 'It don't prove nothing except that when you count up the cigarette smokers in the park, there ain't many.

Most of us use a pipe. Luke Jordan chews.'
Frank cleared his throat. 'Another thing.
We've all heard the talk that Elder Smith had
money hidden in the store, but nothing was
bothered after he was killed, so it wasn't
robbery that the killer was thinking about.'

'Got anything to say?' Bess asked Lux.

'Wouldn't do me no good if I did,' he said
sullenly. 'A hell of a trial, now, ain't it?'

'It's fair,' Bess said. 'If you can disprove
anything that has been said, or give any reason
why Sammy Blue would lie, this is the time to
say it.'

He was sweating, his huge hands knotted on
his lap, his eyes on Bess, then on me, and finally
on the men on the couch. I saw fear in his eyes,
the corroding terror that gnaws at the insides
of a man. Suddenly he lunged out of his chair
and headed for the door. I still had my gun on
him, but I suppose he thought I wouldn't
shoot, or perhaps he was inviting a bullet
because he preferred it to a rope.

I would have shot him if he'd reached the
door, but he didn't. Frank Dance shoved out a
leg and Lux tripped over it and fell headlong,
crashing into the wall. He must have been a
little stunned. Anyhow, Frank was on him
before he could get up. He pulled Lux to his
feet, shoved him against the wall, and rammed
a shoulder into the pit of the man's stomach.

Lux bent forward, his face contorted with
agony as he tried to suck air into his paralyzed

lungs. Frank stepped back, drew a knife from his pocket, and opened a blade. 'You're gonna, plead, mister. You guilty or not guilty?'

Still Lux didn't say anything. Maybe he couldn't yet, but Frank wasn't in a mood to wait. He asked, 'You know where I'm gonna cut you, Lux?'

'Guilty,' Lux whispered, still bent over holding his stomach. 'I shot 'em. The bastards! Better'n me. Better'n anybody else in the park.'

We were silent quite a while, shocked by what he had said. From that moment there was no doubt about what we'd do with him. We all knew, I thought, that we were wrong, at least in part, that we had no legal right to take his life, that the proper course was to turn him over to Veach. But he closed the door on any chance he had for life. Logic told us one thing, our feelings another, and it was our feelings that ruled us.

Bess said, 'What's your verdict?'

'Guilty,' Frank said.

'Guilty,' Kip said.

A moment of silence, then Gil added, 'Guilty.' I nodded.

'Gil, help me saddle up,' Bess said. 'We'll take a horse for Barney.'

They left the house. Frank said, 'Lux, get back to your chair.'

He obeyed, still bent over. Sweat ran down his face. He wiped it away with a sleeve. Then he just sat there, trembling. This was not the

Barney Lux I had known for more than three years. The Barney Lux who had threatened me, who had knocked me down with a blow from his gun barrel and again from his fist. Now his string was wound up, and he knew it. He began to sob, and then he started to beg. 'You can't do a thing like this. Haven't you got any mercy?'

Mercy? A strange word for Barney Lux to use. We just stood there looking at him until we heard Bess call that they were ready.

CHAPTER TWENTY-FOUR

We rode out of the yard and down the lane to the county road and turned east. Bess and Frank Dance were in front, I rode behind them with Lux, and Kip and Gil brought up the rear. No laughter, no words, no sound except the beat of hoofs on the dirt of the road that had been turned hard the last few days by the hot sun.

I had not paid any attention to the weather for several hours, but now I was aware of the sullen mutter of thunder and of clouds moving in from the west. The smell of rain was in the air, flavored by the scent of sage, and it struck me that rain was exactly what we wanted, a regular old gulley washer that would wipe out our tracks. I didn't want to answer Ed Veach's questions.

We crossed Buck Creek, followed the road for another mile or more, then swung north across a stretch of hardpan, going on until we met the creek which angled toward the Big Red from a northeasterly direction. We were on Rafter 3 range now, and from what Frank had said earlier in the evening, I knew this was exactly where we wanted to be.

Barney Lux had not opened his mouth since we'd left Anchor. He'd cracked that one time, but now he seemed composed. He wasn't sobbing or begging, he wasn't even cursing. I figured Lux was a coward because only a coward would have shot my father and Elder Smith the way he had, but now I decided he wasn't. Indifferent to any code of morals, indifferent even to taking human life, but not a coward. At least he was game enough at the finish.

We followed the creek for a quarter of a mile until we reached an ancient cottonwood with limbs bigger than a man's leg. Frank dismounted, saying. 'Stay on your horse, Lux.' The rest of us got down, leaving our horses some distance back of Lux's animal. The moon was overcast, and lightning was working above us. I glimpsed Lux's face, his mouth set hard, bitter and defiant.

Frank took charge and I was glad he did, partly because it was a dirty job, but mostly because I didn't want anyone to think it was personal vengeance on my part. Frank tied a knot in the end of his rope and tossed it over a limb. He worked fast, wanting to get it over with, I suppose.

'Stand up on your saddle,' he told Lux.

He brought his horse in close beside the other animal, tied Lux's feet and hands behind his back, then slipped the noose over Lux's head and tightened it around his neck. He turned his horse and rode off, then dismounted and, returning to the tree, tied the free end of the rope around the trunk of another, smaller cottonwood.

'Got any last words?' Frank asked. 'Any requests?'

'What the hell difference does it make?' Lux said hoarsely. 'You sons of bitches wouldn't do anything for me.'

Frank waited what might have been thirty seconds. I stood staring up at Lux, seeing only a vague figure until the lightning came. My mouth was hot and dry. I had no concept of time. At this moment it seemed to be standing still.

'We'll give you a minute to pray,' Frank said. 'More if you need it.'

'Pray?' Lux said in the same hoarse voice. 'Let her rip. I'll see you all in hell and I'll blackball every one of you bastards when I see you coming!'

Frank turned to Gil. 'You want to give the horse a cut?'

Gil backed off. Suddenly the clouds broke away and the moon came out and I could see his face. He looked as green as moss on the side of a tree. Suddenly he wheeled and walked away. Then he stopped and bent over and was sick.

'I'll do it!' Bess said, and slashed the horse with her quirt.

The animal went out from under Barney in a lunge; his body dropped and turned, his head cocked grotesquely, and then it began to sway like a giant pendulum. I heard the limb creak as his weight struck it. In the moonlight I saw his shadow against the earth, but I could not see the rope, so I had the hideous impression he was hanging between earth and sky.

I walked away and got on my horse. I'd thought I had no feeling about this, that it was simply a dirty job we were compelled to do if we were to survive, but I'd been wrong. I rode slowly, bent over the saddle horn, a terrible sick emptiness in my belly.

We reined up, Frank saying: 'Bess, fix it with Shorty to say you didn't leave your house tonight. Dave, you and Gil do the same with your ma. Kip and me'll do likewise at our place. We know we done right, but Ed Veach ain't gonna see it that way if he gets a notion about what happened.'

We grunted agreement. I guess none of us wanted to talk. Then Frank said something else that I should have thought about, but hadn't. 'Looks to me like there's damned little to choose between the man who buys the killing and the man who does it.'

'We can't get our hands on Vic Toll to hang him,' Kip said.

'But we ain't safe as long as Toll's alive,' Frank said doggedly. 'He can always buy another gun, or use the law to frame us. Hard to tell what he'll do, but he'll do something. Runyan won't, but Toll will. I say he's got to die.'

'How?' I asked.

'I don't know yet,' Frank said. 'Maybe in a gun fight. Gil, you'd be the man to do it.'

'I'll do it,' Gil said. 'But it'll have to be when the sign's right. I can't ride over to Rafter 3 and smoke him down.'

'I don't expect you to,' Frank said, and whirled his horse and rode on.

Kip and Bess went on, too, and Gil and I rode up our lane. We took care of our horses and walked wearily to the house, Gil lagging a step behind me. I was tired in every nerve and bone and muscle. I had never been so tired in my life, I thought, and all I wanted was to lie down and sleep for a week.

There was a light in the kitchen, and I wondered if Ma had slept at all. She had coffee on the stove and was setting the table when I went in ahead of Gil. I suppose she had heard the horses, apparently thinking that there was just one and it was only Gil. She looked up, her gaze on me. I saw shock, and then pleasure. I never dreamed the sight of me would bring that kind of expression to her face.

'Dave!' The word broke out of her involuntarily, and she ran to me and put her arms around me. 'Oh, Dave, you're back!' She hugged me and then she looked up at me, and I knew everything would be all right.

CHAPTER TWENTY-FIVE

A Rafter 3 cowboy found Barney Lux's body and reported it to Vic Toll, who took word to Veach. Toll naturally would deny any knowledge of the hanging, but I suspected Veach was convinced Toll was responsible for it. The sheriff wouldn't know that Lux had been spying and murdering for Rafter 3, and Toll wouldn't tell him that, either.

At least that's the way I figured it, and Veach's nervousness convinced me I was right. He acted like a man who was afraid he'd find the truth and would have to arrest someone he didn't want to. He left the park, apparently as confused as he was after the murders of my father and Elder Smith.

My mother must have known what we'd done, and she must have worried, but she never let on to me. That was one of the changes that had taken place in her. If my father had been alive, she would have fretted about it for weeks, but she didn't bother me with any of her fears.

As far as I know, Shorty Quinn never said anything; but somebody started the story in the park that Lux had sold out to Rafter 3, and now that he was out of the way, there'd be no more killings. I don't know who got the whispering going, but I guessed it was Frank Dance. In any case, what would have been hysteria over the murder of another park man didn't materialize. Instead, everyone was close-mouthed, and it seemed to me there was a good deal of speculation, even suspicion, in the eyes of the park ranchers when we were together for one reason or another.

The body, of course, was brought to the park and we had a funeral. I didn't like the idea of burying Lux in the same cemetery with my father and Elder Smith, but it would have aroused suspicion if I'd raised the point. After Barney Lux's funeral, we forgot the whole business—or appeared to forget it, although I doubt that any of us did.

Gil decided to go to work for Bess, and I hired Kip Dance again. We were deep in the work of the busiest season of the year. We had to plant the spring crops. Because the weather turned abnormally hot and dry, we had to flood our hay meadows. Spring roundup, of course; riding from before sunup to after sundown as we combed the lower slopes of

Campbell Mountain, branding, earmarking, castrating.

Everyone seemed to be satisfied with the calf crop except Matt Colohan. It ran about 95 percent for most of us, and we could look forward to a good beef gather in the fall. If cattle prices stayed up, we'd have the best year since Pa had bought the Big Ten. A gristmill was being built in Buhl, and with the miller talking $1.65, most of us were counting on a little extra money in the fall from our surplus wheat.

Kitsy knew this was the busiest time of year and she understood why my letters were shorter and more infrequent than usual. For the same reason, I suppose, she postponed writing a letter she'd been wanting to write since late April when she'd had her eighteenth birthday. In June I received it.

I had been expecting her to return to the park any day because I thought school would be out, but she'd said nothing about coming back, although I asked her about it in every letter. I couldn't ask Bess because we both avoided the subject. So when Lorna Dance handed this letter to me I stood there in the store and read it, my world was suddenly turned upside down.

Dearest Dave,
    You've been asking in every letter for weeks when I was coming back to the park.

I've avoided answering because I can't come back with things the way they are. I suppose I seem bullheaded to you, and maybe I am. Maybe I'm overproud, but I simply can't come back now. Darling, I just can't.

I suppose I should be grateful to Bess. She practically raised me and she made Anchor pay and she's put money in the bank—I don't know how much, but there must be a lot of it. Now she writes that I'm to go back East in the fall. Miss Crannell, who runs the school I'm attending, says I'll be ready by September if I stay here all summer. But that would be such a terrible waste of money, Dave. It wouldn't make me be any better wife to you.

If I came home now, we would be right back where we were and have to do it all over again. I couldn't stand it, Dave. I won't come back unless I'm your wife. I promise you one thing, Dave. I'll never live in the same house with Bess again. I can live with your mother. I can live in a one-room cabin with you, or a tent, but I'll never live on Anchor with Bess.

Next week end Miss Crannell is taking her girls to Glenwood Springs for an outing. I'm going to be sick. She'll have a fit, but she'll have to leave me. I want you to come to Denver and marry me. I'll have everything ready. I'll even buy my own wedding ring.

If you're coming, wire me from Rock Springs and I'll meet your train.

> Lovingly yours,
> Kitsy

I put the letter back into the envelope and walked toward the door. It was the longest letter Kitsy had ever written me, and the most important. I knew, without her saying it in words, that if I failed her now, she'd be done with me.

I stood beside my bay for a while looking at Campbell Mountain. Funny how you come to a time like this when you know that everything you want, that all your future, depends on what you do. June was no time for a vacation but ... Well, Kip would just have to manage.

I stepped into the saddle and started home. What would I use for money? I still had my $12, and there was a little over $100 left from the sale of the steers last fall. Not enough. Besides the railroad tickets and price of meals on the train, I had to have enough to buy clothes, pay the preacher in Denver, pay a hotel bill, and pay for the meals we would have together. I'd have a livery-stable bill in Rock Springs. I didn't know how much it all would come to, but I knew I didn't have enough.

I rode into the Diamond 8, not really expecting to get the money. I didn't tell Frank why I had to have it. I just said I needed $100, not even being sure that would be enough. He looked at me quite awhile, big and thick-

191

shouldered, his stumpy legs spread, then walked into the house and came back and handed me ten gold eagles.

'I ain't gonna ask you what you're gonna do with it,' he said. 'I'll just take your word that you need it.'

'I'll make out a note,' I said. 'I've got some four-year-olds—'

'Your word's good enough for me, Dave,' he said.

I rode away, thinking how everything had changed in a little over six months. I'd been afraid of marriage that night Kitsy got me out of bed. I wasn't now. I wasn't worried about the future, either. More than that, Frank Dance wouldn't have loaned me the money then, let alone take my word without even a note. I felt good when I thought about it. Everything was going to be all right.

When I got home I asked Ma to fix something for me to eat and to put up a lunch. I said I needed all the money that was in the house. She gave me a questioning glance, but she didn't put the question into words. I got my $12; she brought the steer money, and the little that she had accumulated from the sale of butter and eggs. Not much because she'd given Gil all she'd had when he left.

I rode out to where Kip was working on the ditch. He had a shovel in his hands and he was wearing gum boots and he had mud all over him. He grinned at me when I rode up. I'd never seen Kip so tired he couldn't grin. He said: 'Why don't you move to some country where it rains at the right time? Then I wouldn't have to do this.'

'Good idea,' I said. 'Kip, I'm going to be gone a few days. Think you can make out?'

He leaned on his shovel. 'I figure I can. You don't do no work, anyway.'

'Not any,' I said, and rode away before he asked questions I didn't want to answer.

I put my bay into the corral, went into the house and ate. When I picked up my lunch, Ma asked, 'Know when you'll be back?'

'No. Three, four days maybe.'

'Can you tell me where you're going?'

'Rock Springs.' I couldn't tell her any more than that. 'Good-bye.'

'Good-bye, Dave,' she said, standing at the table, one hand on it, frowning a little.

I saddled the brown gelding my father used to ride. He had more bottom than my bay, and the ride to Rock Springs was a long, hard one. Just as I mounted I saw Si Beam turn into our lane from the county road.

I had the Winchester in the boot and my revolver on my hip, and I had a sudden, crazy urge to shoot the peddler right off the seat of his rig. But I didn't. I rode down the lane to meet him. Before he could say howdy, I yelled: 'Si, back up to the road! I don't know why in the hell you're here, but it isn't for any good.'

He seemed surprised. 'Now, Dave, I've got

some nice things your ma will want...'

'Get out, Si,' I said. 'Go on. Get!'

'What have I done, Dave?'

'You brought Cameron Runyan's offer. I don't know what string you're playing this time, but I'm guessing you're still Runyan's errand boy. You'd better go someplace where he's popular.'

He didn't say another word. He backed up until he reached the county road and then turned upriver. I didn't want to see where he was headed. I didn't care as long as he stayed off the Big Ten.

I made the fastest ride to Rock Springs I ever made, getting off my horse and running part of the time so he wouldn't play out on me. I checked at the depot for the departure time of the next Denver train, left my horse in a livery stable, got cleaned up in a barber shop, and bought my store suit, white shirt, and tie. I barely made the train. I dropped into one of the red plush seats so tired I wasn't even interested in going into the dining car. I put my head back and shut my eyes, and thought about Kitsy.

CHAPTER TWENTY-SIX

The train got into Denver at ten o'clock in the morning. Kitsy was waiting for me. For a moment we stood motionless, suddenly shy

194

with each other, and it seemed to me years had passed since she'd left Dillon's Park. She hadn't changed; she was the same small, fine-featured girl I remembered so well: the sharp little chin with the dimple, the blond hair that showed under the brim of her straw bonnet, and eyes that were the brightest blue I'd ever seen. Yet she had changed, a little fuller of breast, a little broader of hip, an intangible something in the face, all of it adding up to maturity. I was looking at a woman, not a girl.

She cried out, 'Dave! Dave!' and rushed into my arms. I kissed her as she clung to me, and I hugged her so hard I must have hurt her. Suddenly we were aware that people were watching us, some laughing, some just smiling, and all of them thinking, I suppose, that this was June and the time for young people to be in love.

Kitsy turned from me, embarrassed, and picked up a small bag from the floor. 'I've got a cab waiting,' she said, and started toward a street door. I caught up with her and took the bag. When we were outside, I helped her into the cab and got in beside her and placed the bag at our feet. We sat looking at each other. Her hands were folded sedately on her lap, but for some reason my hands were suddenly enormous and I didn't know what to do with them.

I hadn't been in Denver since I was a small boy. It scared me. Not the way I was scared when I saw Sammy Blue riding toward the Harris cabin. It was just that there were too many people, too many rigs, too many streetcars, too many buildings, too many strange noises. I had a crazy feeling I wanted to hear a calf bawl, a lark sing, a jay call as he protested my passage through the pines.

She said, 'Dave, you've changed. I've been trying to figure out what it is. You're not any bigger. I guess you're really thinner, aren't you?'

'I don't know,' I said.

'I've never seen you in a suit before. You're handsome.'

'I feel like I'm in a corset.'

She laughed, and then her face was grave again, her eyes still on me. 'The change is in your face. It's kind of angular. I can almost see your cheekbones.' She paused, then added: 'I know what it is. You've always had the promise of being a man and now you've fulfilled the promise.'

When we reached the preacher's house, Kitsy told the cab driver to wait. Before we went in, she dug a small gold band out of her bag and handed it to me. 'I guess you're supposed to have that,' she said.

I was embarrassed because this was one of the things I should have done. I took it, saying, 'I guess I didn't do a very good job—'

'Hush, Dave,' she said. 'You didn't have any chance to buy a ring that would fit my finger.

Besides, I was the one who asked you to come. I don't know what I would have done if you hadn't.' She stopped just outside the preacher's door. 'You don't feel the way you did the night I got you out of bed? You don't have any regrets?'

'No regrets,' I said. 'No regrets at all.'

'I'm glad, because I know I've been bold; and men don't like bold women. But I couldn't help it, Dave.'

I jerked the bell pull, and the preacher's wife let us in. She was a smiling, pleasant woman who played the wedding march on the organ in their parlor. The preacher performed the ceremony in a great, booming voice, wanting to convince us, I thought, that this was for eternity—which was exactly the way I wanted it.

When Kitsy took off her gray coat, I saw she was wearing a white muslin dress, with soft lace ruffles at her throat and wrists. There was a row of mother-of-pearl buttons that ran from neck to waist, and she wore a gold bracelet on her right wrist. That was all. No garish decorations or jewelry.

On the way downtown to our room in the Windsor Hotel, she told me the bracelet was her mother's, the only keepsake she had. Bess had their mother's gold watch and wedding ring; and Kitsy said, with the first touch of bitterness I'd heard in her voice, 'I guess I was lucky to get the bracelet.'

She instantly smiled the bitterness away. 'I made this dress. It was a spring project. Miss Crannell thought it was just something for summer, but I knew all the time it would be my wedding dress.'

We had dinner in the dining room, then went upstairs to our room. There was so much to talk about, and Kitsy's hunger for news both surprised and pleased me. I didn't tell her about Barney Lux. Sometimes I was ashamed and wanted to forget it. At other times I knew it was the only thing we could have done, and that Lux would have gone unpunished if we hadn't hanged him. But in any case, I couldn't quite bring myself to tell Kitsy about it right then.

The afternoon was gone before we realized it. She stood in front of the mirror and took her hair down. I had not realized how long and beautiful it was. I went to her and put my arms around her and kissed her.

She said softly, 'Dave, you don't know how much and how often I've dreamed about this moment. I thought it would never happen, that it was just something to dream about. I'm ashamed I didn't have more faith, but I can count on the fingers of one hand the times Bess hasn't had her way.'

'I guess I was a little short on faith too,' I said, and hoped she would never find out how short I really had been.

After supper we returned to our room, not

wanting to do anything but be with each other. I said, 'We'll live in our house and see how it goes. I think Ma'll put herself out to get along with you.'

'Dave,' she said, 'I'm not going home with you. Miss Crannell will be back with the girls tomorrow afternoon, and I've got to be there. Just the housekeeper's there now, and I sneaked out. I'm supposed to be sick. I guess I'll be in trouble but I don't care.'

I felt as if she'd slapped me in the face. She sat down on the side of the bed and stared at the floor. 'I don't know if you can understand how I feel or not. I've got a husband and I love him and I know he loves me and will take care of me. I guess I'm afraid of Bess. She's like a big old bull that goes busting through the brush. You get out of the way or you get run over.'

'She can't do anything to you now,' I said. 'You're my wife and you'll live in my house. You won't even have to see Bess if you don't want to.'

'But she'll be our neighbor, and we'll see her at church and the Fourth of July celebration and the Thanksgiving turkey shoot and at Christmas.' She looked up at me. 'When I wrote to you I was thinking about myself, I guess. Bess won't forgive us. If I go back, it would be flaunting her failure under her nose and she'll hit at you someway.'

I shook my head. I couldn't see Bess that way. I said: 'You're mistaken, Kitsy. She's hurt

199

you so much you're prejudiced.'

'I *know* her, Dave. I've lived with her and kept house for her. I know how she thinks and acts and feels. She ran things even when our folks were alive.' Kitsy rose and came to me and took the lapels of my coat in her hands. 'If she would just make a mistake, a bad one. Really need someone's help. If something would humble her...'

'Something has,' I said, and told her about Barney Lux.

She walked to the window. When she turned, I saw she had been crying. She said: 'You go back and tell her, Dave. Let me stay here a little longer—until September. Maybe I'll come back sooner. I'll do whatever you say after you see what she does.'

Kitsy might be right. The thought occurred to me that sooner or later Vic Toll would strike at us with every man he had to get square for Barney Lux's hanging. We were dealing with Toll, not Cameron Runyan, and Toll wasn't one to forgive. If that happened, I would rather have Kitsy in Denver than in Dillon's Park.

'All right,' I said. 'That's the way it'll be.'

She turned to the window and pulled the shade, then whirled and ran to me. 'I love you, darling, I love you. This is our night. Let's not talk about anything else.' She opened her bag and took out her nightgown, glancing over her shoulder at me and laughing. 'Remember when we used to go swimming, Dave?'

I said, 'I remember.'

*   *   *

She went to the depot with me in the morning and saw me off. I knew I would never forget my last glimpse of her, standing straight and proud with the people hurrying around her. A twenty-four-hour honeymoon, a short one, too short, but it was a gem to remember, a perfect island in a stream of trouble.

I would have gone directly to Bess as soon as I reached the park if it hadn't been long after dark. As soon as I was in the house and saw Ma's face, I knew something had happened. She said, 'Ed Veach came out this afternoon and arrested Bess for butchering a Rafter 3 steer. Gil went to town with her.'

So that was the way Toll had worked it. My father, then Elder Smith, and now Bess.

CHAPTER TWENTY-SEVEN

Ma didn't know any details about the difficulty Bess was in, just that Veach had shown up with a warrant and taken Bess to town. Gil stopped by long enough to tell Ma what had happened, then he lit out for town so he'd be with Bess. For one of the few times in my life I honestly admired Gil. He was sticking by Bess when she was in trouble.

I couldn't believe, as Kitsy did, that there had been anything between Bess and Vic Toll. Maybe she had been a little pleased by Toll's attention; maybe even seeing qualities in Toll she wished Gil had; but I was convinced that Bess, in her own way, loved Gil.

Shorty Quinn had told me that Gil was making a fair hand. He'd even put on gum boots and worked all day in the mud flooding Bess's meadows. I remembered what my father had said so often: When a man gets desperate enough he'll find a way to do what has to be done. I think Gil had reached that point.

When Kip came in for breakfast, I asked him what had happened. He had always talked freely to me, but he was close-mouthed on this. He said, 'I dunno, Dave. You go ask Dad about it.'

After breakfast I saddled up and rode to the Diamond 8. Frank was fixing a break in the ditch. He spat into the muddy water that was sluicing through the break in the ditch and making a lake out of his meadow. 'Well, by God, Dave,' he said in a voice that was filled with the same bitter hatred he'd felt for Barney Lux, 'it takes just one rotten egg to flavor a custard, and it seems like we've always got one.'

'Who was it this time?'

'Si Beam. He stayed with Bess, you know. I ran him off the Diamond 8. I guess you done

202

the same. Bess should have, too, but no, she's too bighearted. She fed the bastard and gave him a bed. So what does he do when he gets to town? Swears to Ed Veach that Bess butchered a Rafter 3 steer just before he got here.'

'How'd he know?' I asked.

'Oh, there was a hide hanging on the fence. He found the guts in the corral where we done the butchering, and he found the critter hanging in the meat house.' Frank stabbed the air in my direction with a stubby finger. 'You know what he done then? He spent three days on Anchor eating fresh beefsteak every meal. I reckon it tasted like Rafter 3 meat.'

'It's no crime to put fresh meat on the table. Besides, that hide—'

'He stole the hide,' Frank interrupted. 'They'll cut the brand out and swear we done it. But what's worrying me is that it's a felony to steal a beef. Bess can get anything from one to ten years in the pen. You know you can't find twelve men in the county outside Dillon's Park who ain't afraid to spit in front of Vic Toll.'

'But Bess is a woman,' I said. 'It'd be different if Bess were a man.'

'The hell it would be. They've been taking women prisoners at Canon City since Territorial days. And you know what happened to Queen Ann over there in Craig. She got a hung jury, but what do you think will happen when she gets tried next time?' He shook his head at me. 'No, sir, man or woman,

Bess is in trouble.'

I sat my saddle looking down at Frank, getting a sick empty feeling way down in my belly. I got it whenever I was up against something I just couldn't hack. Frank was right. They'd frame Bess right into the pen. Toll could hire Barney Lux to murder my father and Elder Smith, but he couldn't afford to use that method on a woman, so he'd hired Si Beam to lie in court. The newspapers had howled for years about the rustlers and outlaws that hung out in Dillon's Park. Now this would give them more fuel to burn.

'What'll we do, Frank?' I asked.

'I'm not a smart man, so I don't know,' He wiped the sweat from his face with a bandanna. 'There's something else. That steer was a Diamond 8 critter. The kids made a pet out of him when he was a calf. He got away from us when we were driving up to the mountain this spring, and I've been too busy to chouse him back with the others. Well, Bess came over to see Lorna the other day and she said she wanted some fresh meat, so Lorna said maybe I'd sell this steer. Bess said she'd buy him just to keep from having to fetch one down off the mountain. I helped her and Gil butcher for the liver and heart. I fetched the head home, too, 'cause we like the brains.'

He shifted his weight in the mud, his boots making a sucking noise as he lifted them. 'You remember that fool speech Gil made at a meeting last winter about fighting fire with fire by rustling Rafter 3 stock? Well, the easiest brand to work over from Rafter 3 is the Diamond 8.'

He didn't say it, but I had a hunch that the butchered animal was originally a Rafter 3 steer that had a worked over brand. I couldn't blame Frank, because a steer was small payment for the Diamond 8 grass that Rafter 3 cattle had eaten every winter for years except this last one. But what I thought wasn't the point. Frank might wind up in the pen, too.

'Well,' I said, 'our worry right now is what we can do for Bess.'

'What can we do?' Frank asked.

'We can stick together,' I said. 'When she's tried, Toll will have his crew in town, to scare the jury if nothing else. We can be there, too.'

'You know what that'll mean?'

'A fight. But the way I figure it, Runyan won't stop pestering us until Toll's dead.'

Frank nodded. 'You know I'll back you, Dave, but I ain't sure you'll get every man in the park to go to town that day.'

'They'll go,' I said. 'I figured I'd see them today.'

'I'll ride with you,' he said, 'only I've got to stop this leak.'

'Sure, I may need water sometime,' I said.

I rode the length of the park that day and talked to every rancher from the Diamond 8 to Johnny Strong's place. I talked tough because

205

it was time for tough talk. Either we settled this for once and all or we pulled up stakes and got out of the park. After everything that had happened last winter, there was no middle ground. If Rafter 3 didn't pick a fight in town the day Bess was tried, we would. It was that or let a scared jury send Bess to the pen at Canon City.

I wasn't a popular man that day. Some of my neighbors couldn't see the significance of Bess's trial. Some of them forgot how they'd felt after my father's and Elder Smith's murders; but at last, grudgingly, and after enough arguing to satisfy a Denver lawyer, all but one agreed to go.

Matt Colohan was the one I couldn't touch. He was a little drunk, his big face laced with the red veins, but his whiskey, strong enough to take the lining off a man's throat, wasn't strong enough to make him brave.

'I'm getting out, Dave,' he said. 'My wife wouldn't let me stay if I wanted to.'

'I'll tell you one thing, Matt,' I said. 'If you're still in the park the day Bess is tried, you're going with us or I'm coming after you.'

'I won't be here,' he yelled at me. 'You can count on it.'

That night I wrote to Kitsy. I had decided not to tell Bess about Kitsy and me, at least not for the time being, and I told Kitsy that in the letter. I remembered what she'd said about Bess being humbled. I wasn't sure it would make any real difference, but I'd wait just the same. The trial, whether Bess was convicted or not, would be hard on her. Maybe she would be humbled.

I told Ma about getting married, and it pleased her. 'She's a good girl, Dave. She'll be welcome here.'

I wrote about that to Kitsy, and it made her happy. She had been afraid of the situation just as much as I had been. But Bess's arrest was another matter. Her trouble did not give Kitsy any pleasure. She'd be in Buhl the day the trial started. It proved what I had been sure of all the time: that the ties of blood were stronger than any bitterness Kitsy felt toward her sister.

Bess and Gil were gone for several days. As soon as they got back, I rode to Anchor. I said, 'What can we do for you, Bess?'

Both of them had lost weight, and they looked as if they hadn't slept for days. She looked at me for a long moment, standing straight and proud and unbending. Finally she said: 'Nothing. Nobody needs to do anything for me.'

'You're wrong,' I said. 'If we don't do anything, you'll go to Canon City. Vic Toll will see to that.'

'No, I won't. I'm innocent.'

'Oh, hell!' I looked at Gil. 'What's the matter with her?'

'I don't know,' Gil said. 'She just doesn't think anything will happen to her.'

'What do you think you can do for me?' Bess asked.

'Do you need any money to hire lawyers? Good lawyers, I mean. Expensive lawyers.'

'I've got money,' she said stiffly, 'and I've hired a lawyer—Dan Judson from Glenwood Springs. We went there to see him. That's why we've been gone so long.'

I'd heard of Judson, and he was probably as good a man as she could get. I said: 'There's one other thing we'll do. When does the trial start?'

'July 30th,' Gil said.

'We'll be in town that day,' I said. 'Every man in the park. The first sign we get that anybody's trying to intimidate the jury, we'll go to work.'

Her shoulders slumped, some of the pride going out of her. 'No, Dave,' she said in a low tone, shaking her head at me. 'This is my fight. Mine and Gil's. Not yours.'

'You're wrong again,' I said. 'We'll be there.'

A few days later I heard Matt Colohan had sold out to Luke Jordan, taking Jordan's note, and had left the park with his family.

On the morning of July 29th we gathered at the schoolhouse, every park man but Gil, who had already left with Bess. As we started to town, I think all of us knew that, whatever happened, the next few days would decide our future.

CHAPTER TWENTY-EIGHT

We reached Buhl in late afternoon and camped along the river under the cottonwoods at almost the exact spot where I had camped nearly four years before with my folks. The day was a hot one, and there had been no redeeming shade during the tedious and painful passage across the desert that had been an inferno, so it was with real relief that we bellied down in the gravel at the edge of the stream and drank our fill and sloshed the cool, clear water over our faces.

We took care of our horses, staking them out in the grass between the town and the river, gathered a tall pile of firewood, and stood around arguing about what our course of action should be. My father or Elder Smith would have taken hold; but as it was, none of us had any real status as a group leader.

We were hungry and tired, and all too conscious of the fact that if Vic Toll and his boys were in town we might find ourselves in the middle of a fight before we knew it. I was the only one who wanted to let the townspeople know we were there. I said we'd come to balance any threat Toll would make and the sooner we announced ourselves, the better.

In the end they gave in without me having to

tell them I had another reason, a personal one. I had to know if Kitsy was there yet, and I would have gone alone if I'd had to. First, Frank Dance backed me, then Johnny Strong, and finally the rest of them agreed to go. Hugo March had a prison record, so we delegated him to stay with the horses rather than take any chance of adding to his trouble with the law.

When we reached the courthouse at the end of Main Street, the sun was well down in the west, but the day hadn't cooled. The summer had been dry and hot, with no rain here in Buhl for weeks. The smell of dust and dry weeds was in the air, and I had the feeling that if a wind suddenly came up, every building in the parched town would rattle like a scaffold of bleached bones.

Ed Veach must have seen us from his office in the courthouse. He came out and called to us, standing bareheaded in the sunlight, red in the face and sweating. He looked exactly as he had last fall when I'd come to town with my father; his shirttail hanging over his pants, gun belt buckled under the fold of his belly.

'What are you fellows doing in town?' Veach demanded in a bullying voice.

'Come down off your high horse, Ed,' Frank Dance said. 'We ain't breaking no law.'

'We're aiming to visit court tomorrow,' I said. 'A neighbor of ours is being tried. Remember?'

He backed up, looking us over as if

uncertain how far he could push us, or whether he could push us at all. He said, 'There's an ordinance in this town against packing guns.'

We knew there was such an ordinance, but we also knew it wasn't enforced. I asked, 'Vic Toll in town?'

'No.'

'He will be,' I said. 'You going to take his gun?'

Veach backed up another step. 'I reckon you'd better keep yours,' he said. 'Just don't start no trouble. I don't want this town turned into a shooting gallery. You savvy?'

'Then you'd better see Toll don't start trouble,' Frank said.

'And you'd better see Bess gets a fair trial,' Johnny Strong added.

'You're damned right she'll get a fair trial,' Veach said. 'I reckon you boys never sat in court when Judge Jefferson Brundage was presiding. Nothing formal about him. Chances are he'll call the court to order by pounding the butt of his six-shooter on his desk, but, by God, he's fair.'

Veach started to turn around. I asked, 'Where's Si Beam?'

'I dunno.'

Suddenly it struck me that he might have Bess locked up in his filthy jail. He was halfway to the front door of the courthouse when I asked, 'Where are you keeping Bess?'

'In the hotel.' He turned and looked at me.

'I've got a woman with her. I ain't gonna put her in jail unless she's convicted, but if you boys try to—'

'We won't,' Frank said. 'You just keep her out of that jail.'

I glanced at the sun. After six. All the offices and the bank would be closed. Probably Alec Brady's store would be, too. I'd hoped we would get in town sooner, but we'd spent too much time wrangling in camp. Well, it would be all right, I thought. There were twelve of us altogether, eleven without Hugo March, and it wasn't often that eleven armed men walked down Buhl's Main Street in a bunch. The news that we were there would be all over town within a matter of minutes.

We filed into the hotel lobby. As soon as the clerk, Brown, recognized us, he came out from behind his desk and gravely shook hands all around. He said: 'I'm mighty glad to see you boys. Nobody can scare the judge, but he don't live here. The jury does.'

So we weren't the only ones who were thinking along that line. I asked, 'Where's Bess?'

'In the dining room having supper,' Brown said. 'Where you boys staying?'

'We're camped along the river,' Frank said.

'I'd like to have your business,' Brown said, 'but I guess you're being smart. Toll's reserved seven rooms beginning tomorrow night. Fact is, I don't have enough beds for all of you

212

anyhow. The judge has got a room.' He nodded at me. 'Your brother Gil's got one. So's Bess and her lawyer. A bunch of ranchers from down the river who are on the jury panel are here. You see how it is.'

I nodded, knowing that lack of space wasn't what was in his mind. He just didn't want us in the hotel at the same time the Rafter 3 crew was there. He was right, of course. Our nerves would be tight enough to sing, and there'd be some drinking. It was hard to tell how many of the thin walls upstairs a bullet would go through.

Here again was a line of thinking that wasn't monopolized by one man. We went into the bar. Alec Brady, the mayor, was there, and as soon as he saw who we were he came to us. 'I'm paying,' he said. 'What's your choice, gentlemen?'

We lined up and ordered, then Brady said: 'It's no secret that we've been worried about this trial ever since Bess Nordine was indicted. Rafter 3 will be here in the morning. What will happen then?'

The bartender poured our drinks, but we let them stand. When nobody answered Brady's question, he got impatient. 'All right, all right. You boys didn't come to town for the ride on a day as hot as this.'

'That's right,' Frank said. 'This is a put up job, Alec. We aim for Bess to get a fair trial.'

'And if she doesn't?' Brady pressed.

That wasn't a question any of us could answer, so we turned to the bar and had our drinks. Brady, more impatient than ever, said: 'Now you boys listen to me. I'm the mayor of this town and I'm speaking for it. We've got between three and four hundred people living here, most of them women and kids, and even us men don't have a stake in the trouble between you and Rafter 3.'

I had a sudden feeling Elder Smith was standing at my elbow. I said: 'Wherever little men fight injustice and defeat it, there's a victory for justice for all mankind. You sound as if you're not interested in justice, Brady.'

He blinked, apparently puzzled. The teacher, Rutherford Cartwright, had just come in. He heard what I'd said. 'For a young man, you're unusually philosophical, Munro.'

'Not me,' I said, 'but we had a philosopher in the park who was murdered last spring. I was just trying to say what he would have said if he was alive.'

'Of course I'm interested in justice,' Brady said, 'but I'm also interested in keeping the people of my town alive. I won't have it turned into a target range. If more'n twenty men start shooting at each other, you know what'll happen.'

Johnny Strong hit the bar so hard with his fist that the glasses jumped. 'You better see your folks stay under cover. We've had two men murdered who were as innocent as any of your women and kids. Now one of our women is being tried for something she didn't do. I dunno what's gonna happen, but I know Vic Toll, and I know we ain't gonna stand for him framing Bess Nordine and sending her to Canon City.'

He stalked out, all the rest following him but Frank Dance and me. I asked, 'Where will you and your friends stand if we get into a fight, Mr. Brady?'

He turned his troubled eyes on me, and I remembered that he had spoken up for my father and me last fall after Mort and Blue had been shot.

'We'll stand against the side that fires the first shot,' Brady said: 'but don't let it happen, Munro.'

'We can't promise anything,' I said. 'There's something bigger here than you or me or Bess.'

He got his pipe out and filled it. 'I know that, Munro. Judge Brundage knows it, too. I talked to him this afternoon. None of us likes the things that have happened in this fight you boys are having with Rafter 3, but turning our town into a shambles won't make those things right.'

Rutherford Cartwright nodded. 'I agree with what you said a while ago about justice, but Elder Smith wouldn't claim that wholesale killing serves justice. That's where we're headed, Munro.'

Elder Smith could have argued with him,

maybe found a way out of this mess, but I couldn't. Confused, I turned away and walked into the lobby, Frank following me. All this time I had been thinking that this fight had to be brought to a head, and that Vic Toll and his crew had to be wiped out; but I knew now I was wrong.

I thought about Bess as we walked back to camp through the thickening twilight. If she had any chance, I couldn't see it.

CHAPTER TWENTY-NINE

I sat by the fire a long time that evening after the others had gone to sleep, trying to think of some way out of this without forcing a battle that would, as Alec Brady said, make a shambles of the town. I thought everybody was asleep, but after a while Johnny Strong got up from where he'd been lying with his head on his saddle and squatted beside me at the fire.

'Better go to bed, Dave,' he said. 'You ain't finding no answers here.'

'Thought maybe I would if I stayed here long enough,' I said.

'No, you won't,' Johnny said. 'But there's one thing you've got to do. We're like a rooster with his head chopped off: just flopping around. Come morning, you've got to start giving orders.'

I looked at him in the firelight that flickered on his dark, bony face. I remembered he'd ridden for Rafter 3 years ago. He had the same tough, competent way about him that characterized the cowboys who rode for Vic Toll now. But there was a difference. He'd been gentled by a wife and baby, and I was sure that nobody would ever gentle Toll.

'I can't, Johnny,' I said. 'I'm only twenty years old. I can't tell men like you and Frank what to do.'

'Yes, you can,' Johnny said. 'Remember the day your pa was killed and I told you that you had a lot of Joe Munro in you? That was seven months ago. You've got a hell of a lot more now than you had then. I've seen it grow, Dave.'

I shook my head. 'Give me ten years, Johnny.'

'You haven't got ten years. You haven't got ten days. By God, I ain't sure you've even got ten hours! This is now, Dave. I know most of the boys on the Rafter 3 payroll: a salty outfit as long as Toll's around to do their thinking. Cut off the head of a snake and he ain't gonna do you no hurt. That's the way it is with Rafter 3.'

'You want me to jump Toll?' I asked.

'Hell, no. He'd kill you. He'd kill any of us. I've seen him use his fists and I've seen him draw a gun. Frank Dance is as strong as a stud horse, but Toll would murder him. That's what

217

he wants, Dave. He'll try to bait us into doing the wrong thing.'

'I guess I'm just not bright enough to see what you're driving at,' I said.

'I don't know myself,' he admitted. 'If I had any answers, I'd sure tell you. I just know two things. You've got to figure out the right thing to do and you've got to keep us from doing the wrong thing, or we'll get massacred.'

He got up and walked away. He hadn't helped much, unless pointing out what the wrong thing was. He'd done that, maybe without even knowing it. Before we left the park, I thought that we had to promote a fight if Toll didn't. Now I was convinced that was exactly what Toll wanted and expected us to do.

Rafter 3 could and would roll over us. We had a lot more to fight for than Toll's cowboys, but I had failed to consider the kind of men they were. As long as Toll was alive, they thought they were ten feet tall. He had a way of making them feel that way. Take Toll out of the picture and they were just ordinary cowhands. Months ago my father had said Vic Toll was a legend. Now, more than ever, I knew how true those words were.

And what did we have? With the exception of Gil, we didn't have a man who was fast with a gun. We didn't have anyone who could stand up to Toll with his fists. I named each man to myself and thought about him: Sam Binford,

218

Luke Jordan ... right on through the list. Who could I count on when we got down to the final squeeze? Johnny Strong, Frank Dance, Kip, and maybe Riley MacKay, who would be afraid to run home like a rabbit going for his hole because of what his wife thought.

But Vic Toll, for all of his being a legend, was flesh and blood. He could be whipped. He could be killed. But how? When I finally lay down to sleep, I still didn't have the answer.

We were standing in front of the hotel the next morning when Rafter 3 rode into town, and I was forcibly reminded of all the things I had thought about the night before. Toll, riding in front, completely ignored us. So did his men. We might just as well have been eleven clods lined up on the boardwalk. That was part of the game. We weren't worth noticing.

But you couldn't help noticing Vic Toll any more than an insignificant bit of steel can help being drawn to a powerful magnet. He must have finished growing ten years ago, but every time I saw him he looked bigger and more formidable than he had the time before, his great chin more powerful, his hooked nose more domineering. I'd thought the same thing the time I'd seen him behind Elder Smith's store, I'd thought it when he'd ridden up with his crew Thanksgiving day, and I thought it now.

The courtroom wasn't large, and we weren't able to sit together in a block as we had hoped.

Ed Veach was up in front with Si Beam. I knew, then, that what I had suspected all the time was true. He'd been keeping Beam under cover. As soon as the trial was over, or when he had given his testimony, Beam would light out of Marion County on a high lope. He knew what we'd do if we ever caught up with him.

Toll led his men into the courtroom a minute or two after we sat down. He went right up the aisle to the front. The two rows on the left were filled, but that didn't stop Toll. He said, 'We'll take these seats,' and I'll be damned if every one of those men didn't get up and let Rafter 3 have them. I glanced at Johnny Strong, who nodded at me. Everything he'd said the night before was confirmed by this one bullying act.

Gil was in the front row a couple of seats from Veach. Bess and her lawyer, Judson, sat at a table on the other side of the railing. As I expected, Bess hadn't prettied up for the occasion. She was wearing her riding outfit, a black, split skirt and a dark green blouse. As always, her hair looked a little wind blown. But she sat straight-backed, holding her head high and proud, and to me she was a strong, handsome woman. In her way she was just as formidable as Vic Toll. I couldn't help thinking what a couple they would have made.

The judge entered the courtroom from his chambers and stalked to his desk. He said, his voice tremendous for so small a man: 'The court of this judicial district is now in session.

First case is the State versus Bess Nordine. The defendant is charged with the larceny of one steer belonging to the Rafter 3 ranch owned by Cameron Runyan.'

He paused, and drawing a long-barreled revolver from his waistband, laid it on the desk. Ed Veach said that was what he might do, but I hadn't believed it. There was something ludicrous about the whole thing, but no one laughed. The first man who laughed would have been held in contempt, and I was sure Brundage would have made it stick.

For a full minute we sat in silence, the only sound in the room coming from a fly lazily buzzing against a window. Johnny Strong and I were in the back, so I was unable to see the faces of any of our friends, but I could see the backs of their heads, their necks, and their shoulders. Every one of those men was gripped by a muscular tension that was a sort of paralysis. Then I looked at my hands, clenched so tightly the knuckles were white.

I wasn't any better than Frank Dance and Riley MacKay and the rest. Johnny Strong, sitting beside me, was no different. We were all thinking the same thing, I knew: that Bess Nordine had become more than the defendant in this trial; she was a symbol of all we had fought for and were still fighting for. If she went to prison, so would Frank Dance, and after that it could happen to any of us.

But it was more even than that. Here it was,

pinned down in this little courtroom: our future, our lives, our property, and even our rights as citizens. Either Vic Toll made a mockery of law, or Bess went free. To me it was that simple.

'I want to say a few things before this trial gets under way,' Brundage said. 'My court is never a formal one. The reason is simple: justice is often lost among legal technicalities. Our criminal laws are designed to protect the innocent as well as society in general. My duty is to see that this purpose is carried out.'

The judge paused, and Luke Jordan clapped, his big hands making a tremendous racket in the crowded room. Brundage pounded the butt of his gun on the desk, glaring at Jordan.

'If that happens again, I'll clear the courtroom.' Brundage laid the gun down. 'I have been told that there is a great deal more at stake in this case than appears on the surface. I have also been told that I can expect an outburst of violence from the side that loses. The sheriff has not seen fit to disarm you men who are here as spectators on the ground that this is still a frontier community, and a gun is as necessary for a man's survival as his horse. I understand that; and now you men who are here had better understand something. I will not tolerate outbursts of any kind while the court is in session. What's more, I will shoot the first man who attempts to turn this trial into an ordeal by violence.' He sat down. 'Call the first juror.'

I felt like clapping, too. I was convinced that no other judge in the state ran his court the way Jefferson Brundage did, and I was equally convinced that no other judge could cut through legal red tape and get down to the basic elements of justice the way Brundage would. For the time and place, Judge Brundage was perfect.

The lawyers took the entire morning to pick the jury. I like the way Daniel Judson performed. He was a tall, lantern-jawed man who might just now have ridden in off the range. He belonged in this country; he talked our language, and I was convinced that the jury would believe him if any lawyer would be believed.

Loyd Mack was the prosecutor, a short, stocky man who was inclined to be overbearing at times, and that, I felt, would work in our favor. But the little confidence I had began to fade as I watched the growing number of men who sat in the jury box. The solid men like Alec Brady and Rutherford Cartwright were dismissed. The ones who were retained were like the barber, Scissors McGuire, who would turn whichever way the wind blew.

The jury, as finally selected, was composed of five townsmen and seven ranchers from down the river. I couldn't really object to any of them, but at the same time there wasn't a man in the bunch I felt we could count on.

When court was recessed at noon, I waited until Frank Dance came down the aisle and walked out with him. I asked, 'What do you think?'

Frank was not a man who ordinarily showed his feelings. Now he looked at me, and I saw more misery in his face than he had ever let me see before, more even than last Christmas when I found him in our house with my father's body.

'We're whipped, Dave,' he said.

'Not yet,' I said. 'They haven't even started—'

'I tell you we're whipped,' he interrupted. 'Just look at them boogers on the jury. Who are they watching? Vic Toll, that's who.'

I couldn't say anything to that because he was right. We walked in silence to the Chinaman's place at the end of Main Street. We ate there, and when we got back to the hotel the jury was finishing dinner. I stood in the archway watching for a minute. Toll's bunch had the three tables in the back of the room. None of them tried to talk to the jurors, but the room was filled with their loud voices and laughter. Maybe I imagined it, but it seemed to me Toll was throwing his weight at the jury without committing an overt act of any kind.

I turned and walked toward the door, jerking my head at Johnny Strong, who motioned to Frank Dance. A moment later we were all standing on the boardwalk.

I said to Johnny, 'All that damned jury needs is just to see Vic Toll.'

He nodded, his eyes hard. 'Got any ideas, Dave?'

'No.'

'Better get some,' he said. 'When do you figure it'll go to the jury, Frank?'

'Tomorrow afternoon, I'd say.'

'That's what I figured.' Johnny looked at me. 'You ain't got much time.'

'Better go back to the courtroom,' I said wearily. 'I've got to meet the stage.'

'Why?' Johnny asked.

'Kitsy's coming in.'

'That's a good enough reason,' he said, and walked away, the rest following.

I watched them go, slow anger beginning to burn in me. I asked myself, 'Why me?' I had no answer except that I was Joe Munro's son. The jury returned to the courthouse. So did Bess, Gil, Mrs. Veach, and Judson. The Rafter 3 crowd moved past, ignoring me, and I felt a little easier after they had gone. I was alone. It would be easy enough to pick me off. But I was small fry, too small to bother with.

The stage was due at one, but it was late. I waited in the hot sunshine, my thoughts turning to my father who had come to Dillon's Park a drifter, a man who had never been able to get his roots down and make his dreams come true during all those years of wandering. But in three years he had done it. He had become the most solid man in the community, the man Frank Dance and Johnny Strong and the rest turned to just as they turned to Elder Smith for another kind of leadership. How had he done it? I didn't know, but I did know that if it hadn't been for Vic Toll, my father would still be alive. We'd hanged Barney Lux, but Vic Toll hadn't been touched.

Kitsy was on the stage, as I knew she would be, slender and pretty in a jaunty blue bonnet and a long, tan duster. I kissed her, hard, a little brutally, I guess, but not intending it to be that way. I just couldn't help it. To me, Kitsy was a thin ray of sunshine in a long, dark tunnel.

'I'm glad you're here,' I said. 'I'm awfully glad.'

'It's where I've wanted to be for a long time,' she said.

I took her suitcases into the lobby, she signed the register, and we went upstairs to her room. She was tired and hungry, but she couldn't eat. 'I've got to be in the courtroom this afternoon. I wrote to Bess I was coming and she wrote that I had to stay.' She tried to smile but couldn't quite manage it. 'So this is it, one way or another. Have you told her about us?'

'No,' I said.

'It's all right. It's my job.' We left her room, and when we were out on the street she asked,

'How's it going?'

'Bad,' I said.

'You're tied up,' she said, 'all over in hard little knots. I felt it the minute you kissed me. Is it just Bess?'

'No,' I said. 'It's Vic Toll. I've got to kill him.'

'And make me a widow at eighteen?' she asked.

I didn't say anything. There wasn't anything I could say.

CHAPTER THIRTY

Si Beam was testifying when Kitsy and I reached the courtroom. Every seat was filled, so we had to stand in the back. Frank Dance turned his head, and, seeing Kitsy, rose and motioned for her to take his seat, and stood beside me.

Apparently Beam had already told the bulk of his story. Now Loyd Mack was going back over his testimony, making him repeat the relevant parts. He stood a few feet from Beam, teetering back and forth on his heels, his thumbs stuck through the armholes of his vest.

'You stated you are a peddler by profession,' Mack said, 'but on this occasion you were in Vic Toll's employ as a detective when you visited Dillon's Park.'

'That's right,' Beam said. 'I've made trips to Dillon's Park every spring and fall for years. I'm well known there for that reason, but if a stranger visited the park the rustlers would have been on their guard—'

'Objection.' Judson jumped up. 'No one in Dillon's Park has ever been proved to be a rustler.'

'Objection sustained,' the judge said.

'I mean that if there was any rustlers in the park,' Beam said, 'a stranger would be more likely to make them cautious, but they wouldn't think anything about me.'

'You stayed with Bess Nordine?'

'That's right.'

'You were given free run of the ranch?'

'Yes. Miss Nordine was riding with her crew every day I was there.'

'Now there is no question about this hide you found on the fence?'

Beam snorted. 'I said awhile ago there wasn't.' He pointed to a hide that hung over the railing in front of the jury. 'That's it. The first time I saw it the Rafter 3 brand was there, all right. I left the ranch after dark and took the hide with me. When I got to town, I gave it to the sheriff. That was the first time I knew the brand had been cut out.'

'You believe the accused cut the brand out?'

Judson was up again. 'Objection. That's opinion; it's not evidence.'

'Objection sustained,' the judge said.

'Phrase your questions more carefully, Mr. Mack.'

'Now, then, you stated that there was a carcass in the meat house that had been recently butchered?'

'Yes. And we had fresh beefsteak every meal while I was staying at Anchor.'

'But you weren't able to verify the brand by the earmarks?'

'No. I hunted all over the place and I couldn't find the head.'

'It is your opinion, then, that the accused hid the head to prevent—'

I heard grumbling from the front of the room where Johnny Strong and Luke Jordan and the rest sat, but before the judge could pound for order Judson was on his feet, gesturing wildly in Mack's direction. He shouted, 'Your honor, any boy reading law to prepare himself to pass the bar examination knows the difference between evidence and opinion. We've had instance after instance where the prosecution has planted suspicion in the minds of the jurors by this method. I submit that this procedure is unethical, morally dishonest, and points to the fact there is no real evidence against the defendant. I move that this case be dismissed.'

'Motion denied.' Brundage looked at the jury. 'You will disregard anything the witness says which is strictly a matter of opinion.'

Mack kept Beam on the stand for another

half hour, making him repeat the same thing over and over in different words. It was so monotonous it was painful. Then I thought I understood. Beam's testimony was all the evidence the state had. In the end it would be his word against Bess's, and against Frank's and Gil's, who butchered the steer.

A mighty slim case! It proved what I had thought all the time. Vic Toll was confident he didn't need evidence to convict Bess, that the jury would be afraid to bring back any verdict but guilty. I studied the faces in the jury box and I had a terrible feeling Toll was right. There were twelve uneasy men on that jury. All of them from time to time glanced at Toll. I suppose they were wondering what he was thinking, and what he'd do to them if they went against his wishes.

Even with the windows open, the courtroom was stifling. Frank Dance poked me in the ribs with an elbow and jerked his head at the door. I nodded and followed him outside. We were both jumpy, but Frank was worse than I was. He kept walking around, mopping his face with a red bandanna.

'What'd I tell you, Dave,' he said, 'about them jurymen watching Toll?'

'They're watching him, all right.'

Frank threw his cigarette away. 'I'm next. I'm going crazy, Dave, thinking what it would be like in Canon City, and what'll happen to my family. Kip's the only one who can make out by himself.'

'What'll happen to all of us if they convict Bess?' I asked.

'I dunno,' he said slowly. 'Reckon I was just thinking of myself.'

'Maybe you'll be next,' I said, 'but the rest of us are in line; so are the people in town. The little ranchers down the river are in the same boat. Maybe those boys on the jury are thinking of that.'

Frank rubbed his palms against his shirt, and shook his head. 'Hell, maybe I'm just boogery. Let's go back.'

When we returned, Judson was cross-examining Beam. 'You testified that you visited Dillon's Park every spring and fall as a peddler. Did you always stay with Bess Nordine when you were in the park?'

'Yes,' Beam answered. 'When her folks were alive, I stayed with them. After they died, Bess asked me to continue making her ranch my headquarters whenever I was there.'

'You had been accepting her hospitality for years,' Judson said. 'You went there this time with the express purpose of securing evidence to send her to the penitentiary. What kind of a man are you, Beam?' Judson turned away, his face and voice showing the magnificent contempt he had for Si Beam. 'That's all,' he said, and returned to his table.

Loyd Mack howled his objection, but Judson had made his point. Beam was a small man, but now he was less than half the size he had been a few seconds before.

Gil was the next witness. He was sworn in and sat down. I didn't have the slightest idea why Mack had called him. I didn't think Gil did, either. He'd look at Bess and then at Mack, squinting against the late afternoon sunlight coming through a west window. Even where I stood in the back of the room, I could see the sweat running down the sides of his face.

'It is my understanding, Mr. Munro,' Mack said, 'that Rafter 3 cattle have wintered in Dillon's Park for years up until last winter. Is that correct?'

'Yes.'

'According to my information, there was a meeting of the Dillon's Park Cattlemen's Association in the schoolhouse during the winter. This meeting was called to discuss plans for keeping Rafter 3 cattle out of the park. Is that correct?'

Gil swallowed, and glanced at Bess. 'That's right,' he said.

'Now, Mr. Munro,' Mack said, 'will you tell us what you said at that meeting?'

Gil half rose from his chair and sat down again. He looked at Bess, who was more worried than I'd ever seen her, then turned his gaze to the judge. 'Do I have to answer that question?'

Judson was on his feet again waving at

232

Brundage. 'Your Honor, I object. This line of questioning has nothing whatever to do with the case that is being tried.'

Mack reared back on his heels and slipped his thumbs into the armholes of his vest again. 'Your Honor, this has everything to do with the case. I propose to show that a conspiracy existed in Dillon's Park to destroy the Rafter 3 by rustling its stock.'

'Your Honor,' Judson shouted, 'you can't destroy an outfit by stealing a single steer and that is what Miss Nordine—'

'Your Honor,' Mack yelled, 'I propose to show intent.'

Brundage pounded the desk with his six-shooter. 'I'll have you both dismissed from this case if you yell at me again. I may be old but I'm not deaf. All right, go ahead.'

Barney Lux must have reported to Toll what Gil had said at that meeting. At least, Loyd Mack knew what Gil had said or he would never have put the question. Gil had his tail in a crack, all right. He couldn't lie—not about a public statement he'd made before every rancher in Dillon's Park.

I expected Gil to cave, but he didn't. Mack said smugly, 'All right, Mr. Munro, answer my question.'

'All right yourself,' Gil snapped. 'I'll answer it, but I've got something to say first. Last summer was a dry one, and we knew we didn't have enough grass in the park—'

'The question, Mr. Munro!' Mack said. 'What was it you said at that meeting?'

'I'm telling you.' Gil gripped both arms of his chair, glaring at Mack. 'We refused to let Rafter 3 cattle winter in the park because we didn't have the grass to spare.'

'Your Honor,' Mack wheeled to face the judge. 'The question can be answered directly without the explanation the witness insists on giving.'

'Answer the question,' Brundage said.

'I said we had to fight fire with fire,' Gil said. 'I said that if it wasn't profitable for Rafter 3 to winter their cattle in the park, they wouldn't do it. If we rustled their stock, it wouldn't be profitable, but we never had to go that far because they didn't shove any of their cattle into the park.'

'Your witness,' Mack said to Judson, and sat down.

Judson rose and walked to where Gil sat in the witness chair. 'Do you know why Rafter 3 cattle were not driven into the park as they had been in the past?'

'We never tried to keep them out before,' Gil said. 'This time we did, so they worked another angle. Two men were murdered—'

'Objection,' Mack said. 'That's irrelevant to this case.'

'Objection sustained,' the judge said.

Judson hesitated a moment, and then said, 'That's all,' and returned to his chair beside

Bess.

Mack didn't have any other witness to call, and the judge said that would be all until tomorrow morning at nine. The crowd headed for the door, but I jammed my way against the current until I reached Kitsy. I said, 'Has Bess seen you?'

'I don't think so,' Kitsy answered.

I heard Vic Toll's big voice boom out above the hubbub, 'Long as that bunch is in the park, nobody's cattle will be safe.'

'How many do you suppose they got?' one of his men asked.

'I dunno,' Toll said, 'but it sure explains why our tally's short.'

I felt Kitsy stiffen in rage. I stood beside her, my hand on the butt of my gun while the Rafter 3 crew moved past us to the door. I stared at Toll, but he ignored me completely. I was like a bug under his foot, I thought. Kitsy and I worked our way to the front. Bess was surprised when she saw Kitsy, but she held out her arms and they hugged each other.

Bess said, 'I told you to stay in school.'

'I couldn't stay away when I knew you were in trouble,' Kitsy said.

'I'm not in any trouble Gil can't get me out of,' Bess said, but her tone lacked conviction. 'Let's get out of this oven.'

She walked out with Mrs. Veach, Gil a step behind her.

'I wanted to tell her about us being married,'

235

Kitsy whispered, 'but I couldn't. Not now.'

'No,' I agreed. 'Not now.'

Johnny Strong and Frank Dance were waiting for us in front of the courthouse. They shook hands with Kitsy, then Johnny said to me, 'Got any ideas yet, Dave?'

'No.'

'Time's run out on us,' he said. 'Toll was talking big when he left the courthouse. He ain't the kind to talk big unless he's getting worried, and if he's worried he'll move.'

'What'd he say?' I asked.

'He's gonna run Gil out of town,' he said. 'He's gonna run him so fast his heels will be smokin'.'

'Did Gil hear?'

'Sure he heard,' Johnny said. 'He was walking past with Bess and Mrs. Veach when Toll said it.'

I looked along the street to the hotel. Bess, Mrs. Veach, and Gil had disappeared, but the Rafter 3 crew was just going into the Belle Union. This was the first time Vic Toll had tipped his hand. I wasn't sure he was worried. Maybe he'd planned it this way all the time. He had Gil boxed so he had to fight or run. If he ran, he lost Bess. If he fought, he'd die. That was the way I thought Toll had it figured. If Gil died, the jury was bound to hear, and the news would be a warning.

Shorty Quinn was standing about fifty feet from us, talking to Luke Jordan. I called,

'Shorty.'

Shorty Quinn started toward us. I said: 'Johnny, you get two double-barreled shotguns and some shells out of Brady's store, and meet me in front of the hotel. Frank, you run herd on our boys. Keep them together in case we need them.'

They moved away, not understanding but not questioning me, either. When Shorty reached us, I asked, 'Was there ever anything between Bess and Toll?' He started to tell Kitsy he was glad she was back, but he never got started. He looked at me as if he thought I was crazy. I said impatiently, 'Were they in love?'

He drew back a fist. 'By God, Dave, I ought to—'

'Hold on Shorty,' I said. 'Tell him, Kitsy.'

'I saw them kissing each other,' she said. 'It was the night of the meeting when Gil made that talk about rustling Rafter 3 cattle.'

Shorty swallowed. I wasn't sure he believed her, but he wouldn't call her a liar.

I said, 'He was with Bess Thanksgiving day, too. After the turkey shoot.'

Shorty began rubbing a boot toe through the dirt. He said, 'There's something you don't know, Dave, but it answers your question. Toll rode in on Christmas day right after we heard about your pa getting killed. Bess met him in front of the house. She had a Winchester. She called him some names I never heard her use before. I thought she was gonna kill him before

237

he finally got it through his head he'd better get out of there if he was gonna stay alive.'

I understood it then, or thought I did. They had been trying to use each other; but, being the kind of people they were, they were bound to fail. That was something Toll would not forget or forgive. He'd get square with Bess by sending her to prison, and he'd kill Gil because he was the man Bess had picked.

'Stay out of trouble,' I said to Kitsy. 'Shorty, you see that she does,' and I started toward the hotel on the run.

CHAPTER THIRTY-ONE

The hotel lobby was empty when I got there. I took a quick look at the register, saw Bess's room number, and ran up the stairs. I knocked on the door. Mrs. Veach opened it and started to say no visitors were allowed, but I jammed past her. Gil was standing at the window.

'Gil,' I said, 'remember the time you won the $40 at the turkey shoot last Thanksgiving?'

He didn't answer. He stood with the late afternoon sunlight falling against his back so his face was shadowed, and I could not see his expression. I wasn't sure whether he'd run or fight, but if I'd been gambling on it, I'd have given odds he'd run. I moved to one side so I wasn't facing the sun. Then I saw his face. He was in hell, knowing what he ought to do and afraid to do it.

Bess sat on the bed, her hands folded on her lap. She said: 'Dave, I'm not going back to the park if the jury acquits me. Gil and I have been talking about it. He wants to buy a horse ranch somewhere and settle down. I guess that's the thing to do.'

If she wanted to get my mind off Gil, she succeeded. I realized again how much I admired her. Stubborn, strong-minded, independent: she was all that and more. If she could, she would have buckled on a gun and faced Vic Toll herself. Kitsy thought Bess had to be humbled, but now, as I looked at her, I knew that nothing on God's earth would ever humble Bess Nordine, not even a guilty verdict from the jury.

'You've got to go back to the park,' I said. 'We need you.'

'Nobody needs me,' she said. 'Nobody but Gil. I think $15,000 is a fair price for Anchor. I'll have Judson draw up the papers. You can borrow half of that amount from the bank and give me my share. Gil and I will need it when we leave here. You can run Anchor and the Big Ten together. You'll have a good outfit, Dave, one of the best in the county.'

She had it all figured out. She wasn't asking me. She was telling me. The thought that Kitsy might object apparently never entered her mind. That's the way Bess always had been and

239

the way she always would be.

I brought my gaze back to Gil. Bess knew Toll had to be taken care of. She was too practical to think anything else, and she was leaving it up to Gil because there was nothing else she could do. I was sure she knew the risk he would take. If Toll killed him, her life would be ruined, but I was confident she would never let anyone know.

'Remember that turkey shoot, Gil?' I asked again, and he nodded. 'Frank said you were our best fighting man, and you said if he wanted any fighting done, to just bring 'em on.'

'He remembers,' Bess said.

'And one time Bess said she didn't want any help but yours,' I said. 'You told her she'd get it when the sign was right. This is the time, Gil.'

He had been staring at the floor. Now he looked at me as if he thought I was crazy. 'You want me to fight twelve men?'

'No,' I said. 'I'll take care of eleven, but Toll's your job.'

Gil looked at Bess. 'He's been eating loco weed. He can't handle eleven men.'

'I don't know how he aims to do it,' Bess said, 'but I think he can. You've always underestimated Dave. So have I.'

'Come on,' I said impatiently. 'We can swing it now. If we wait, Toll will jump you, and chances are I won't be able to help. But if you jump him, you've got an edge.'

'Dave's right.' Bess got up and went to him
240

and kissed him. 'You were a long time growing up, Gil, but I waited until you did.'

She turned away from him and stood looking out of the window. I walked to the door and motioned for him to follow me. He did, not because of anything I had said or done, I thought, but because it was what Bess expected him to do.

As we went down the stairs, I said: 'I know how you feel. I felt the same way when I was in the Harris cabin and I saw Sammy Blue coming. But I'm alive and Blue's dead.'

He didn't say a word. He just licked his lips and went with me down the stairs and across the lobby and into the street. I'd said that to give him confidence, but I hadn't. Then I remembered I didn't have any confidence when I faced Sammy Blue. I just tried my damnedest and won, and that was all Gil could do.

Johnny Strong was waiting for us with two double-barreled shot-guns. He handed one of them to me along with a handful of shells. I dropped the shells into my pocket, broke the gun and saw that it was loaded. I snapped the gun shut and started across the street angling so we'd reach the corner of the saloon and not be standing by a window or door.

The way I saw it, there was a good chance we could pull it off. Toll was the pusher. As far as I knew, no one had ever challenged him. I was confident that the possibility we might open the game would never occur to Toll or his men.

The element of surprise was the one slim factor that might tip this thing in our favor.

When we reached the corner of the saloon, I said, in a low tone: 'I'm going in and brace the whole outfit. Johnny, I'll give you a minute to get around to the back and come in that way. We'll have them between two fires, so I don't figure any of them will pull a six-shooter against a pair of scatter-guns.'

Johnny had plenty of sand in his craw, but he didn't like the smell of it. He said, 'There's too many of 'em, Dave.'

'We can do it,' I said. 'We've got to give Gil a chance for a fair fight with Toll.'

'He'll get that anyway,' Johnny said.

'Gil's not sure about that,' I said. 'There's another angle to think about. Once Toll's dead, we're going to run the whole crew out of town.' When he still hesitated, I said: 'Johnny, you wanted me to give the orders. All right, I'm giving them.'

He started along the side of the building, bending down when he went under a window. I looked at Gil. Nothing flashy about him now. No green silk shirt or calfskin vest. No loud talk. No brag. His lips were squeezed together so tightly they were white. His face had a lean, hungry look about it; the muscles at the hinges of his jaws bulged out as if they were the halves of an oversized walnut.

Suddenly it occurred to me that Johnny was right. This was a crazy scheme. Gil wasn't the only one who might get killed in the next few minutes. The Rafter 3 men weren't going to just stand there and look at me, shotgun or no shotgun.

Gil was a reluctant hero, but so was I. I knew I had to go in then or not at all. I couldn't wait until I was sure Johnny was coming through the back door.

'I'm going in,' I said. 'You stay by the batwings. Soon as I get that bunch separated from Toll, you come in.'

He nodded, and I started for the front door, bending down so I'd be under the one window between the corner and the batwings. I wasn't sure Gil would ever come through that door, but I couldn't back out. Frank Dance and the whole park bunch were watching me. So was Kitsy. And probably Bess. She'd be watching Gil, too. He knew it. That was my one real hope.

I went in fast, both barrels cocked. Vic Toll was the nearest to the door. The rest were lined out along the bar almost to the far end. I had counted on surprise and I was right. Twelve hound dogs would never expect a rabbit to turn on them and fight, and that was just about the way this stacked up to them.

'Stand pat,' I said, angling toward the opposite wall.

They swung around to face me. I had never seen as many surprised faces in my life as I did right then. One man about halfway down the bar, the fellow who called himself Slim Jim, started dropping his hand toward his gun. I yelled at him: 'Hold it or I'll blow your God-damned head off! Somebody will get me after that, but it won't help you any.'

He froze. So did the rest of them. Then Toll found his voice. 'What the hell is this, Munro? Trying to commit suicide?'

'No, but the first man who tries for his gun will,' I said. 'Toll, stay where you are. The rest of you move to the other side of the room.'

Toll laughed. At that moment he looked bigger and tougher than he ever had. A human life meant nothing to him. I doubted that he knew what it was to be afraid. He said: 'Do what he says, boys. I'm a mite curious to see what he's up to.'

I was trying to watch all of them, and I just couldn't do it. I was panicky, then, panicky enough to have done something foolish if they hadn't obeyed Toll's orders, but they did. They started drifting across the room, and then there were several I couldn't watch because they were hidden by men between me and them.

I didn't have enough eyes to watch the back door, but I heard Johnny call, 'Don't try it, Les! If Munro don't get you, I will.' In all my life I had never heard a sweeter sound than Johnny Strong's voice.

We had them lined up along the wall then. Johnny said: 'Shuck your gun belts. Slow and easy. Just let 'em drop. Some of you boys might decide to get brave.'

They unbuckled their gun belts and dropped them, a few cursing us, most of them grinning as if this was a joke. I wondered what Toll was doing. I couldn't risk taking my eyes off the crew to look at him. If Gil didn't come through the door, Johnny and I were both dead men because Toll had his gun and we were standing with our backs to him. Then I heard the whisper of the batwings flapping shut, and Toll's jeering voice, 'Well, I'll be damned. This rooster's growing a set of teeth.'

I turned then because I had to. Gil had stopped just inside the door, his right hand hovering over his gun. His face was white, but he wasn't trembling. He had complete control over himself just as he'd had last Thanksgiving when he'd shot at a walnut.

I looked at Toll. He was staring at Gil as if he expected him to run, but Gil didn't run. Then Toll made his play. The shots came, close together, one, two, the thunder of the explosions slamming into each other and running out across the room until the echoes died. Gil didn't move. He held the gun at his side, smoke drifting out of the barrel.

Toll had been hit hard, the bullet slamming him back, but he was still on his feet. He dropped his gun, and now he gripped the bar; but even Vic Toll could not defy Death. Suddenly he began to wilt. His hand slipped off the bar and he went down. He reached for the footrail, gripped it, and tried to pull himself up, but the strength wasn't there. He went slack, his head dropping against the floor and making a faint, thudding sound.

I motioned to the bartender. 'Take a look at him,' and turned back to face the men along the wall.

'He's dead,' the bartender said.

I said: 'You boys are leaving town. We don't care whether you keep on working for Rafter 3 or not. Just stay out of the park and keep your stock out.'

Gil dropped his gun back into the holster and moved away from the door. We marched the Rafter 3 crew into the street. Frank and the rest were waiting, their guns in their hands. Frank said, 'We'll take care of 'em.'

'Toll's dead,' Johnny said. 'Gil shot him.'

'I figured he did,' Frank said, 'or you wouldn't be pushing this bunch around. They look like a bunch of dehorned yearlings to me.'

'They're staying out of town till the trial's over,' I said.

'You damn' betcha they are,' Frank agreed. 'Get moving, boys. You're taking a ride, right out to Rafter 3.'

Townsmen appeared along the street. Alec Brady, Rutherford Cartwright, and Ed Veach, too, but he didn't butt in. Cut off the head of a snake, Johnny Strong had said, and it won't hurt you. He'd been right. The Rafter 3 crew didn't look like a very salty outfit as they

246

headed for the livery stable.

I went back into the saloon. Toll was lying where he'd fallen but Gil wasn't in sight. The bartender pointed to the back door. When I reached the alley, Gil was bending over, sick. I waited, leaning the shotgun against the wall. I didn't feel much better than Gil. He retched for a while; then when it was over, he got his bandanna out and wiped his face.

'Hell of a note, now, ain't it?' He tried to grin, but it was more of a grimace than anything else. 'You reckon Pa would have been proud of me?'

'Sure he would,' I said.

He told me a lot with that one question. All this time he'd wanted Pa's respect, and he knew he'd never had it. The things Ma had done for him just hadn't been enough.

We walked along the alley to the end of the street. By the time we reached the hotel, the Rafter 3 men were mounted. I went on through the lobby with Gil and up the stairs. He was weak, panting by the time we reached the landing.

Bess was waiting in the doorway of her room. 'Get out,' she told Mrs. Veach. 'I'm not going anywhere now.'

Mrs. Veach obeyed. Bess put an arm around Gil and took him into the room and shut the door. I turned just as Kitsy came running up the stairs, calling, 'Dave, oh Dave!' I caught her in my arms and kissed her, and then she put her head on my chest and cried, and I held her that way a long time.

CHAPTER THIRTY-TWO

A shadow was lifted from Buhl the day Vic Toll died. I felt it that evening before Kitsy and I went up to our room; I felt it again when we went down for breakfast in the morning. I saw it in the faces of people in the lobby and in the dining room, especially the jurors. I sensed it in their voices and the way they laughed. Yesterday there had been no laughter.

After we finished breakfast, I waited in the lobby while Kitsy went up to our room. Alec Brady came out of the bar, smiling as he moved toward me. He said, 'You'll be headed home before noon, Dave. The law says they've got to finish the trial, but it'll be just a formality.'

He was the mayor, and he spoke for the town, and in many ways he represented the best that was in the town. He teetered back and forth on his heels, thumbs stuck through the armholes of his flowered waistcoat, a cigar in one corner of his mouth. All was right with the world as far as Alec Brady was concerned, and I could not keep from comparing him to the frightened man we had talked to in this very place the first evening we were in town.

'I hope we'll be able to get home tonight,' I

248

said. 'We've all got work that's pushing us.'

'Sure you'll get home,' he said confidently. 'And another thing: you won't have any more trouble with Rafter 3. I know Cameron Runyan. All this strong-arm stuff was Toll's idea. After what's happened, Runyan won't send another man like Toll to ramrod Rafter 3. He couldn't find one anyhow. When the Lord made Toll, He threw the mold away.'

Kitsy came down the stairs then, so I nodded at Brady and we left the lobby. Clouds were in the sky, and it seemed to me the air was cooler by twenty degrees than it had been yesterday. Children played in the street, and even at this early hour women hurried along the boardwalks toward Brady's store to do the shopping they had not done the day before. Buhl had returned to normal.

Just as Brady had said, the trial was little more than a formality. Apparently Si Beam had left town. At least, he wasn't in the courtroom. Daniel Judson put Bess on the stand, then Gil, and finally Frank Dance. They testified the butchered animal was a Diamond 8 steer. Loyd Mack's cross-examination was perfunctory. Even as he asked questions, he had the look of a man who knew he was beaten. Judson's and Mack's final arguments were brief. So were the judge's instructions to the jury. It wasn't out five minutes when it brought in a 'Not guilty' verdict. We stood up and cheered, the townspeople as well as those from the park.

We shook hands with Bess who acted as if she had known all the time it would be this way. Kitsy threw her arms around Bess and kissed her and cried a little. Bess plainly thought Kitsy was being silly about the whole business. That was exactly like Bess, but Kitsy was acting the only way she could. I was proud of her because it proved what I'd always known, that she had a heart as big as her head. She told Bess we were married, and Bess, surprisingly, accepted it without argument.

We were all in a hurry to get home, but Kitsy and I had to go to the bank. I asked Frank to fetch my horse, and sent Kip to the livery stable to get a horse for Kitsy. We weren't in the bank more than a few minutes. Judson had prepared the papers. I borrowed $8,000, enough to pay Bess for her half of Anchor, and still leave me all I'd need to return the $100 I'd borrowed from Frank and keep us going until we sold our steers in the fall.

As we left the bank, Bess said: 'Gil and I are getting married this afternoon, but we'll stay in Buhl until I get my clothes. Kitsy, I want you to pack them up and send Shorty to town with them tomorrow.'

'Why don't you come to the park and pack them the way you want them packed?' Kitsy said. 'You can tell everybody good-bye.'

'No,' Bess said. 'I'm not going back to the park. I don't want to tell anybody good-bye.'

She smiled at Gil. 'We're starting a new life. We'll never look back, will we?'

'No,' Gil agreed. 'We're looking ahead.'

When we reached the hotel, Kitsy ran up to her room to change to her riding clothes. She had a small trunk and several suitcases, but we couldn't take them because we didn't have a rig. Shorty could get them when he came to town tomorrow with Bess's things.

Kip brought a horse from the livery stable. Frank and Johnny Strong and the rest had come from the river, Frank leading my bay. There was a deal of shaking hands, everyone telling Gil he'd done a job the day before. For a while I could see the old Gil. All he needed were his green silk shirt and calfskin vest with the silver *conchas*; then he turned to Bess and saw the way she was looking at him. She whittled him down to size with that one glance.

I remembered that time last fall when my father and I were fixing the corral gate and Gil rode in from Anchor and told Pa to saddle up, that they were going to drive the Rafter 3 cattle off our range. It seemed a long time ago, and it had been, judging by what had happened. And I remembered thinking that I hoped Gil got Bess. It would serve him right.

Now he had her. This was his moment; he had succeeded in doing the only thing he had ever actually set out to do. I wondered how it would work. Well, I wasn't going to worry about it. Gil had what he wanted and I had what I wanted, and from now on our lives would follow separate paths. I wasn't at all sure we would ever see each other again.

Suddenly Gil turned to me. He said, as if it had just then occurred to him, 'Dave, I won't be seeing Ma. Tell her good-bye for me, will you?'

'I'll tell her,' I said. 'Write to her this time.'

Bess said: 'He will. I'll see that he does.'

She would, too, I thought. Frank asked: 'Why ain't you coming to the park, Bess? Don't look like good sense, you and Gil striking out—'

'It makes sense to me,' Bess said sharply. 'I'm just not going back.'

And that was all there was to it. Kitsy came out of the hotel. She kissed Bess, and then Gil. She said, 'I'd like to stay for the wedding—'

Bess interrupted. 'No, you go along.' And that was the end of that.

I didn't kiss Bess and she didn't offer to kiss me. I shook hands with her, then Gil, and helped Kitsy into the saddle. I mounted, and we headed for the park, the rest of them falling in behind us. A mile of two out of town, Johnny Strong caught up and rode beside Kitsy and me. He said: 'I thought yesterday you were crazy, putting all your chips on Gil the way you did. But he did the job.'

'He wasn't the one who did the job,' Kitsy said tartly. 'I'm sick and tired of people bragging on him. Dave was the one, going into

252

the Belle Union all by himself. And you too, Johnny.'

'Sure, I know,' Johnny said, 'but what I'm trying to say is that we've had Gil sized up for years. I didn't think he had it in him.'

'You know what Pa always said.'

Johnny shook his head at me. 'Guess I don't know what you mean.'

'He used to say that if a man got desperate enough, he could do what had to be done. That was the way I felt when I came out of the courthouse and you said time had run out for us and we had to do something. I think Gil felt the same way. He knew he couldn't ever face Bess if he didn't go through with it, and marrying Bess is the only thing he ever really wanted.'

'That's something else I can't figure out,' Johnny said.

'I've heard Elder Smith say you have to accept love but you don't explain it,' I said. 'I think it's true.'

'Maybe so,' Johnny said.

After that we rode in silence, Johnny dropping back to ride with Frank Dance. In late afternoon we reached the place where we had turned off the road with Barney Lux. Some things, I thought, were so deeply burned into your memory that you never forget them no matter how much you want to. Hanging Barney Lux was one. Finding my father's body Christmas morning was another. Shooting

Sammy Blue. And that long, terrible moment yesterday afternoon in the Belle Union when I stood with a shotgun in my hand facing the Rafter 3 crew. I hadn't been at all sure Gil would come through that door, not nearly as sure as I had let Johnny Strong think I had been.

We splashed across Buck Creek, and Dillon's Park lay before us. Funny how memories rush back into your mind at certain times. This was such a time, and I knew Kitsy and I faced a new life, just as Bess had said it would be for her and Gil.

I was remembering the first day we had seen Dillon's Park. My mother had come against her will and Gil had been sullenly silent; but there had been a look on my father's face I would never forget as he looked. Campbell Mountain on one side, the high cliff across the Big Red on the other, and the long valley ahead that was Dillon's Park. No, I would never forget that look. This was his dream come true; this would be his home, and here his roots would go down.

I suppose the same expression must have been on my face. Kitsy leaned toward me, her voice very low when she said: 'Dave, I know how you feel. We're home, but do you know how I feel?'

'No, I guess not,' I said.

'Happy,' she said. 'Just awfully happy.'

We reached the end of our lane. Luke Jordan

called, 'Look out for us one of these nights.'

And Riley MacKay said, 'I've been wanting to go to somebody else's shivaree ever since I went to my own.'

'Forget it,' I said. 'We're old married people now.'

Johnny Strong snorted derisively. 'You're not getting out of it, boy. Don't ever think you are.'

They rode on, all but Kip, who went on up our lane, and Frank, who reined up. I could hear laughter and talk from the others coming back to us until distance muffled the sound. Frank sat his saddle, looking at us, his wide face grave, his great hands folded over the horn. He wasn't a philosophical man, or a particularly thoughtful one, but now I saw he had something on his mind, so Kitsy and I waited.

'Everything's changed,' he said, 'one way you look at it. Changed the minute Vic Toll died, and it changed some more when the jury let Bess go. Changed for me right then 'cause I've been in a hell of a sweat, thinking that if they sent Bess up I'd be the next.'

'Brady says Runyan will never hire another man like Toll,' I said.

'Hope not,' Frank said, 'but whether he does or not, geography ain't changed a damned bit. You're still sitting on the anxious seat 'cause you're here at the head of the park.'

'I'm not worried, Frank,' I said. 'We found

something out yesterday. We worked together, and if it ever comes up again, we'll keep on working together.'

Frank nodded. 'That's right. I reckon geography ain't so important. I'm thinking it don't make no difference what Runyan throws at us. We'll handle it. We've got him whipped.'

'That's the way I figure it,' I said. 'Say, I'll bring that money I borrowed—'

'Any time, Dave, any time,' he said, and rode away.

Kitsy and I turned our horses up the lane. I saw my mother in the yard, facing the sun, her hand shading her eyes. Then we waved at her and she waved back.

Kitsy asked, 'What more could we ask, Dave?'

'Nothing,' I said. 'You can't ask for anything more when you've got it all.'

We hope you have enjoyed this Large Print book. Other Chivers Press or G.K. Hall & Co. Large Print books are available at your library or directly from the publishers.

For more information about current and forthcoming titles, please call or write, without obligation, to:

Chivers Press Limited
Windsor Bridge Road
Bath BA2 3AX
England
Tel. (01225) 335336

OR

G.K. Hall & Co.
P.O. Box 159
Thorndike, Maine 04986
USA
Tel. (800) 223–2336

All our Large Print titles are designed for easy reading, and all our books are made to last.